Back Home is, by far, my favorite of her works. The story is angsty and heartbreaking and full of hope and healing. It is so poignant and beautiful. It's a book full of ups and downs and is near impossible to put down once you start reading. It's a story of unrequited love and sacrifice. It's a work of beauty. I was enthralled from beginning to end... I absolutely adore Back Home. In fact, it's a book I'd recommend to just about anyone. It's heartbreaking and hopeful at the same time. The story that Scott tells is a hard one of love lost and love found. It's a bittersweet and poignant story, but it's also beautiful, sweet, and perfect. I highly, highly recommend Back Home by RJ Scott.
~ *Joyfully Jay*

Books by RJ Scott

Ellery Mountain

The Fireman and the Cop
The Teacher and the Soldier
The Carpenter and The Actor

Single Titles

Moments
Back Home

Back Home

ISBN # 978-1-78651-893-4

Cover Art by Posh Gosh ©Copyright 2016

Interior text design by Claire Siemaszkiewicz

Pride Publishing

Published in 2016 by Pride Publishing, Newland House, The Point, Weaver Road, Lincoln, LN6 3QN, United Kingdom.

Pride Publishing is a subsidiary of Totally Entwined Group Limited.

BACK HOME

RJ SCOTT

Dedication

Always for my family.

Chapter One

"J, are you coming?"

Jordan Salter jumped a little and glanced up from his work, refocusing tired eyes that had been intent on minute hand work on a three-by-three post of kiln-dried walnut. He widened his eyes fractionally in the gathering evening gloom, blinking and attempting to make sense of the new focus of his concentration. The ache behind them was the icing on the cake—a by-product of the nagging headache that had tracked him all day and the need to concentrate on creating the intricate detail work that he was determined to finish. He closed his eyes briefly, gritty exhaustion in them, and he let out an almost incoherent, "Wha...?"

"You said you were going to be finishing early today."

"Wha...?" *What is it with people interrupting my work?*

Whoever it was in the room with him flicked on the overhead light, courtesy of the electrical work that had been completed and signed off today. Jordan winced.

"It's past eight and you're still here?"

Jordan blinked steadily—if it was eight o'clock then why the hell was Ben standing in the house? He should have gone home two hours ago. Come to think of it, why was Ben dressed to the nines in his Sunday jeans and a clean shirt? Jordan remembered last seeing his friend and colleague in overalls, working on wiring. Ben Craig was the only subcontractor they called on and then only in an emergency.

"You said to come back for you. To remind you about the party." Ben was clearly and deliberately speaking in words containing minimal syllables, and he spoke slowly enough

7

that Jordan could absorb the words. Tension stiffened the older man's stance, and his expression schooled itself into a frown. What was he supposed to remember? Suddenly, through the fatigue, the memory clicked into place. The party. Hayley's party. She was twenty-two today, and he'd been invited to join the Addisons and associated friends at The Olive Garden for dinner.

"Shit."

"In it, big time," Ben muttered, walking across the kitchen and, almost as if he couldn't help it, sliding the palm of his right hand over the unwaxed, still-dull brown wood that Jordan had chosen for the newel post. Fingertips barely touching the surface, Ben traced the grain and nodded. Jordan looked from the wood to Ben and back again, mind working feverishly to keep his focus on the fact that he'd promised to be at the party.

"She'll be pretty," Jordan offered, wondering if he was coming across as defensive even as he dismissed the thought and focused on the beauty of the wood.

"She'll polish up well," Ben agreed. "Walnut was a good choice."

"I just get..." *Involved*, he finished in his mind. Engrossed to the point that he felt no weariness until his attention was broken. From intricate carved details on newels to the hand-turning and intricate inlay work for chair backs, Jordan had always been mesmerised by the forms he could create. The patterns and the curves under his fingers had always been inside the wood, as far as he knew. Able to find the faintest of grains, he would sand and shape and polish, thinking of nothing except the beautiful wood beneath his touch. Once he saw the purpose of each piece of wood, and had paid attention to the shapes buried in each piece, he laid out the finished product in his head. Giving his thought to the raw potential in front of him, he focused on having the wood's final shape match the completed mental image. He often didn't know where to start, but when he was in the zone, when each tiny cut made the beauty of the wood show in striations of pale brown and gold, he couldn't snap himself out of it.

Tonight wasn't the first time over the last few months that he'd forgotten something, nor would it be the last. Jordan was tired, and he felt years older than his twenty-nine. He commonly put in eighteen-hour days. First had come the hard physical work on the larger aspects of renovation, then the labour-intensive detailed finishing woodwork on Mistral House had consumed him.

Recession had hit the construction industry hard, and he was the sole remaining staff member of Addison Construction. AC'd had no choice — people had had to be let go, and he was finishing this contract on his own, with just Ben in and out for things he couldn't do, electrical being one of them. When Jordan was working on the final touches in a renovation, he sank into the process, the carving and staining and completing his only reality. Intensely involved and completely cut off from the rest of the world, such things as birthday parties and promises to attend them didn't exist.

AC needed to flip Mistral House as soon as they could — the very existence of Phil Addison's company depended on the cash flow realised from the sale of the home. Added to the stress of the need to finish, he'd had little more than three hours sleep last night, and he was into his nineteenth hour working today.

He glanced back down at the smooth wood, the texture of the newel satiny and solid beneath his fingertips, judging that he only had a quarter hour, maybe half, and this part of the detailed intricate work would be finished.

The kitchen cabinets, each custom made, were solid walnut, generations of growth in the sturdy wood. Jordan's elaborate detailing accentuated the highlights and lustre of the wood's deep honey tones. Jordan had created a pedestal, circular-topped kitchen table and four chairs as well, and the rails complemented the other wood in the room. The kitchen was the crowning glory of the carpentry in this house renovation and a source of great pride to Jordan.

He had, after all, done most of the work single-handedly, since Phil had become too ill to work alongside him. The kitchen was his baby, and he just needed to finish the detailing — tonight. Ben stood, waiting for an answer if his subtle shifting from foot to foot was anything to go by.

"I'll be there before they cut the birthday cake," Jordan compromised softly. Softly because he half hoped that Ben wouldn't hear and, if Jordan seemed to ignore him, would just give up of his own accord and leave. Jordan didn't need the inevitable lecture as to why he should be with the Addisons, that it was important he was there for Hayley, because he was all she really had left in the way of a brother.

Lady Luck however, was not smiling down on Jordan Salter. Ben heard him and started to work up a good head of steam.

"You go nowhere. You do nothing outside of working. You work all hours God sends us. Do you have a freaking death wish, son?" It was that single word — son — that broke through Jordan's barriers. There was affection in Ben's voice — affection and concern. Maybe he should stop working. Maybe Ben had a point.

"Ben..." He turned slightly, determined to talk, then had to jerk to catch a hammer he had knocked with his arm.

"God damn fool. You're an accident waiting to happen." Ben's eyes narrowed as he sized up Jordan from that new perspective. And he clearly didn't like what he saw.

"I'm not far off finishing." There was steel in his voice, even he could hear it, and he winced inwardly. Ben didn't deserve his disrespect. However tired he felt, he should at least try to be polite.

"You're not far off killing yourself." Ben's normally calm voice held something new. A level of panic had replaced a little of the anger. Jordan dealt with Ben the only way he knew how, by dismissing Ben's concerns out of hand, not giving the electrician any room to carry on the conversation.

"For God's sake, Ben, I'll be along in an hour."

"Half an hour," Ben snapped back at him. Temper coiled in Jordan, but how could he lose it with Ben, when the older man really *did* have reason to worry? And Jordan knew it.

He didn't think he'd ever felt so low on reserves, so damn drained, but Ben didn't know the full extent of the shit that Addison Construction was in. He wasn't aware of the debt that sat at the bank, the check that the Mistral House was just about to cut for them only just covering the deficit. The timing had to be perfect. They were coming to inspect in two days, and he had so little to do to finish. Jordan let Ben keep talking, ignoring it mostly for his own sanity, until Ben reached his peak then just as suddenly stopped.

Jordan frowned at the sudden silence. Silence with Ben was always a bad thing.

"Brad wouldn't want you working yourself to death just to get to see him sooner." Ben's words were weighted with sadness, and he said them so firmly, not backing off one inch from his opinion.

Guilt, anger, temper — all three churned in Jordan's gut, then came a sudden maelstrom of grief. The overwhelming feelings he felt when he thought about the man he had loved and lost were something he ruthlessly pushed down. He locked them away, behind walls of stone. Fuck. Exhaustion was letting the hidden emotions through. Ben should leave well enough alone. Why did he even have to mention Brad, tonight of all nights? Couldn't he see that Jordan was busy trying to save the company from going bust?

Ben looked at him with such mute understanding in his lined and weathered face that Jordan felt the temper in him begin to dissipate. He banked the fire of his anger as much as he could, channelling it to fuel his stubbornness. He didn't have any response to Ben's statement. Really all he wanted to say was that, yes, maybe he did want to join Brad, that somehow dying would make everything easier. Maybe if something did happen to him it would be for the best. He was insured big time, and his will specified everything would go to his surrogate family, the Addisons, and that would clear all the debt and then some. He turned on the small jigsaw he'd been using earlier to do more shaping on the newel post. The high whine of the machinery made talking impossible, and it was the only way he could stop himself from giving in to anything other than the determination to finish this damn house. His throat was thick with emotion, and his thoughts writhed — tangled and tied in all manner of what-ifs in his head.

Ben should never be forced to bear the brunt of that horror. Deliberately, Jordan turned his back on Ben. In no uncertain terms, he declared the conversation over and returned to concentrating on finishing the work. He caught a glimpse of the worried expression on Ben's face, but he ignored it. And he heard the quiet "This is getting too dangerous" Ben muttered to himself as he left, but he ignored that too. Jordan only relaxed when he sensed that he was alone in the room and glanced over his shoulder to confirm that the door no longer framed his friend. Gone with him was the air of disappointment and growing concern that had surrounded the older man.

With a hefty exhalation of relief, he turned back to the work at hand, trying to find his balance, desperately attempting to connect to the skill that was inside him, not wanting to ruin everything now. Working with his hands, creating beauty out of the wood, comforted him and centred him. Kieran had once called him an artist…

Jesus. Where had that thought come from? First Brad and now Kieran? This was one hell of a night for ghosts and memories to choose to haunt him.

Trying to calm his anger and the roiling misery inside him, he was able to push through the complete exhaustion, the last, stuttering pulse of adrenaline forcing him towards the finish line. The bone-numbing, bone-deep tiredness verged on paralysis and was causing his eyes to half close. His muscles, operating with an overload of lactic acid, howled with pain. Jordan knew that he'd pay dearly for the abuse in the morning. At least the pain would be eased a bit by the satisfaction of creating the final invoice for the two hundred thousand they were owed.

Ben's words rattled in his head — Jordan was too far past exhaustion to be able to block them. Damn him for talking to Jordan now about Brad. Hayley's birthday meant that the anniversary of Brad's death was only days away, the dark anniversary of a nightmare that had yet to lift. His concentration slipped, and he caught himself just in time to stop the wickedly sharp blade from carving a hole in his hand. Through the fog of weariness, one lashing flicker of reality shot through. Jordan felt rather than heard his frustrated sigh.

That had been too close, much too close. He was being an ass. Insurance money or not, he wasn't suicidal and he would be no good to the Addisons or to himself if he managed to destroy his most important tools — his hands. It was way past time to stop.

Jordan stretched up and took a step backwards, his legs cramping, sore and tight from being in the same position for so long. The pain and a momentary weakness in his left leg caused him to stumble to the left. Attempting to catch himself, he somehow managed to tangle his foot with the cable to the saw, causing his hand to slide up against the thin blade. The pain was instant, and the power cut off just as quickly.

He'd managed to yank back as the blade had touched his skin. But the damage had been done. The blade had sliced into his wrist and the fleshy part of his hand. The injury was so deep he could see bone. The first shock of pain was so intense it sent him stumbling backwards until he crashed into the stool he'd been using.

Something in the back of his mind screamed, *Stop the bleeding! Get help!* But he didn't know how to do either. Shock rendered him mindless. Blindly he lurched to rest his forearm on the stool and tried desperately to get the gaping wound closed using his uninjured hand.

Blood surged between his fingers and down his forearm,

slithered across the seat of the stool, and ran down the nearest leg before it combined with the sawdust on the floor into a horror of reddish wood paste. Jordan, head light with the deeper onset of shock, pain making it almost impossible to think, knew with absolute certainty that losing blood as fast as he was meant he could die. He released his hold on the wound, scrabbling for his cell phone, which he'd left lying on the side of the saw table. He cursed as it slithered away from his blood-wet hand.

"Son of a bitch. Fuckin' son of a bitch," he muttered over and over, the smell of blood—his blood—making him nauseated. He grabbed again for the cell, managed to reach it and flipped it open.

His vision greying and his eyes closing, somehow, from somewhere, he remembered that he needed to put pressure on the injury. Hitting redial was all he managed before the cell dropped to the floor as red with blood as his hand. The floor rose to meet him in a haze of wood and grey, and he collapsed to the ground, his injured hand mashed into his shirt. He rolled, his arm under his body, and knew he would soon lose consciousness in a twisted maze of blood and wires. He knew it. He watched the scarlet spread more slowly but still relentlessly from under him as the blood, his life, saturated sanded wood floors and seeped between smooth bare floorboards.

In the swirling grey-black, Jordan's thoughts became dazed. *Maybe this is okay. Maybe it doesn't matter.*

It wasn't going to be long, then, if he was lucky, he would have the chance to tell Brad how sorry he was. How sorry…

And the world disappeared into dark.

Chapter Two

"Kieran, there's a call for you on line three," Tamsin called across from her desk. He had been concentrating on a whole raft of t-crossing and i-dotting for documents on his desk.

Kieran didn't receive calls at work. He had yet to reach the lofty position of full architect, and an encroaching social life was frowned upon. He was biding his time as a junior, albeit a junior with five years' experience and a degree from Central Saint Martin's College of Art and Design in London. His job at Drewitt-Nate was to file papers, check figures, speak to land registry and make coffee, whilst being paid a pittance to learn at the feet of the partners.

"Who is it?" he replied, reaching for the phone.

"Someone with an accent," Tamsin said offhandedly with an exaggerated shrug.

An accent could mean anything. It could be Austin from the art department, or Emily from the council's building control department, both of whom had fairly broad Scottish burrs. It could even be his best friend, Evan, with his Vermont vowels, but then he normally texted or instant messaged. Shuffling the papers on his desk to one side, Kieran pulled out a notepad and a pen, and clearing his throat, pressed the button for line three.

"Kieran Addison," he said. The line was quiet, no words, just an empty silence. "Drewitt-Nate Architects, Kieran Addison speaking. Can I help you?" There was a burst of noise on the line, and the distance from which the call had travelled caused a faint echo.

"It's me." His sister's voice suddenly spilled over the line.

"There's been an accident. It's Jordan."

"Hayley—"

"I don't know what to do, and dad is so ill. They didn't want me to tell you but—Kieran, please come back home." His sister's voice broke as she sobbed, and fear gripped him as hysteria and desperation peppered every word. "We need you here! Please, please come back home…"

Kieran Addison hadn't exactly been expecting a call from Hayley. They hadn't talked much on the phone, if at all, in the last few years, especially not since the funeral. They still emailed occasionally, jokes and stories mostly, but the important thing was that they kept in touch. They still *knew* each other. She was his sister, after all, and they were still close.

There was just too much pain for both of them. When they started talking, they also began thinking all over again that where there had once been three, only two remained. Gradually, almost as if they had an unspoken agreement, they had allowed the weekly calls to drift away into no calls at all.

Email was safer. Texting was safer. They hadn't actually physically talked since Kieran had returned home two years earlier to be with the family as they'd buried Brad. Brad's death had cast a shadowy, grief-filled chasm between them, and they had not recovered to the point where they could share their thoughts.

A few minutes later, Kieran replaced the handset, his head spinning. He had agreed to go home. After six years, he was going back to Cooper's Bay and to the family he had left behind. Back to all those memories, all those mistakes, all that grief. He bent his head, faintly aware that Tamsin hovered at his side like a fox on the hunt, asking him what was wrong.

He said nothing. The news he'd been given snarled in knots and tangles in his mind. The decision to go home had not been one he'd wanted to have to make this quickly, least of all without a lot of thinking. Bracing his hands on the desk, he pushed himself to his feet, the chair rolling away until it thunked to a dead stop against the half wall of the next cubicle.

Blinking, he looked at Tamsin. For once she seemed slightly concerned about someone other than herself. Or she might have sensed a good bit of gossip in the air and readied herself to pounce on it. She even patted Kieran's forearm, a peck of a pat, as if he might respond with too much emotion. It was disconcerting to have her hand on him, and he brushed her off with a murmured, "I'm okay."

She didn't give up, tagging after him down the side corridor that led to the canteen and the restrooms. Tamsin may have viewed the limits on personal space as fluid, but even she didn't follow him into the men's bathroom. Kieran slipped into one of the stalls rather than standing at a urinal, and at last, he had a few moments peace to try to understand what he'd just been told.

His dad had a heart condition, Jordan had been in an accident and Addison Construction was on the edge. *What the fuck*? When he'd left Vermont, the company had been going strong. What the hell had Jordan done to cause it to, apparently, suddenly fail? For a few more minutes he sat where he was, mind shifting quickly through the things that needed to be done in London before he could get on an aeroplane and head for home. Then, still stunned, he left the stall and made his way to one of the small sinks.

Kieran splashed water on his face, the icy cold tingling on his shaven skin, and, without consciously deciding to do so, he slipped off his suit jacket and dumped it in the next sink over. When his tie joined the inexpensive jacket and he stood only in shirt and pants, he was more Kieran Addison, son and brother, than Kieran Addison, rabbit hutch paper pusher.

He needed to speak to the partners. His review last week had been more than good, excellent in fact. They had suggested it might be time for him to contribute to some of the smaller design projects, a slowly opening door that promised him what he had always wanted. With his entire being, Kieran wanted to be able to design and build structures that would last as long as the building he could see from the window near his desk. The city's network of medieval streets proudly displayed a stunning variety of both old and new buildings. Old solid brick houses sat next door to the glass banks of modern finance headquarters, a stone's throw from the Square Mile, a minute's walk from St Paul's Cathedral.

He would be giving everything up if he had to go home. *Had to go home?* He didn't have to go home. Going home was the right, the only thing, to do, regardless of his reservations. It was an easy decision to make in the end. Knotting his tie and slipping his jacket back on, he approached the partners to request a break to attend to family business. For two weeks, maybe three, at the most four.

They deliberated, offered him two weeks with the expectation that he would return. He thanked them, thought inwardly that two weeks was fine, that it was actually pretty generous. If his inner voice was snapping that two weeks with his family was too long, then he squashed the thought.

* * * *

Kieran had booked a ticket to the incongruously named Burlington International Airport, and packed his entire life in two suitcases and a carry-on.

Evan McAllister, the reason he'd moved to London in the first place, had driven him to Gatwick, and they'd been sitting for a long time in the outside concourse waiting for the flight to be called.

"I have a month left on this contract with the design company." Evan ran a hand through his spiky red hair, wrinkling his nose as an indication of exactly what he thought of the company he worked for. "I'll be heading back home for a visit."

"You won't need to. I'll be back here soon," Kieran offered

immediately.

Evan simply shook his head, elaborating on what he'd just said. "If you get there and you decide you need to stay there, then I'll be home in a month. Let me know."

Kieran eyed Evan, who had been his best friend since they were five, and, not for the first time, felt enormous love and affection well up inside him.

He buried himself inside Evan's comforting, completely encircling hug. "It's okay. You won't need to come after me. As soon as I sort this, I'm coming back to London," Kieran said, although he realised he'd said it without a lot of conviction. At those words, Evan pulled back, his expression thoughtful as he touched Kieran gently on the cheek. His friend was wearing the most serious expression Kieran had seen in a long time.

"You won't be coming back to London." Evan didn't sound disappointed, more adamant.

"I need to," Kieran protested quickly. "My job—"

"Your job—your career—are nothing you can't have in Vermont."

"I can't stay there…" He couldn't finish the sentence. He didn't have to. Evan knew him well enough to know what was unspoken.

"With what happened with Jordan, you left so you wouldn't see him every day. But, really, you should never have left with me in the first place."

Back then, when the world had held so many possibilities, when his brother had still been alive, when he'd needed to avoid Jordan like the plague for fear of letting his feelings for his brother's lover become known, London had glowed, a bright shining hope. Evan had had his own reasons for leaving Cooper's Bay—he had a controlling father who didn't want a writer son with a gay best friend, and the chance of a place at a prestigious college was a way for Evan to escape. Kieran had applied to the same college with its highly regarded architecture program—a solid place at a good college, following his best friend to a new city. It was a brand new start and a place to meet guys — men, not boys, and anyone that wasn't Jordan. He'd had a chance to wash away everything that had gone wrong. So Evan had ended up studying his creative writing, and Kieran, architecture, at the same college, an institution that was prestigious and respected in both their specialities. They had shared a small apartment, split the costs, partied hard and studied harder. It had been perfect.

"I needed it." Kieran was firm in what he was saying. Hell, he had needed more than anything to get away from the temptation that was his brother's lover. Evan nodded in agreement — he knew the whole story. Then he pulled him in for a backslapping hug.

"I know."

"Evan —" *I'm going to miss you. How am I going to do this without you having my back?*

"Hey," Evan said low and even in his ear, "I think it's time for us both to go back home."

* * * *

The flight was interminable. May sixth segued into May fifth without Kieran sleeping. The seating was cramped and the air hot, and Kieran couldn't settle to read or watch the in-flight movie. Instead he found himself staring out of the tiny rounded window at the vast skies, settled into that uncomfortable headspace where he was reliving all his best and worst memories. Half a day was consumed in crossing the Atlantic, changing flights on American soil, then finally landing back at Burlington.

His already grief- and fear-dazed mind barely able to function, he followed the crowd through Arrivals. No small amount of apprehension tossed and churned in his stomach. Baggage claim was easy enough — his bags came off first — and as he had passed through customs at the previous changeover, he just went through the motions, not realising what he was doing. He ran down the concourse to the place where family and rides waited for incoming travellers and looked around for Hayley. She'd promised to be there to meet him, and when he saw her, he wrapped her in his arms and questions tumbled from his lips unbidden.

"How long has Dad been this ill? Where are the rest of the employees? How is Mom? Is Jordan okay? What happened? Why did no one call m—?"

Hayley finally shook her head firmly and stopped his babbling mid-word.

"We'll talk in the car," she said simply, picking up his carry-on and leading him out the side of the building. Early morning sun glinted off the windows in the archways that housed the main concourse. It was promising to be a fine and clear late spring day. The car was on level four of the second parking area and standing at the wall afforded a wide view of the airport. The edge of one of the far runways and the terminal that was mildly busy with arrivals and departures were so much smaller than the airport in London. He knew it was only called an international airport because it had flights to places like Canada, but small as it was, it was still his first taste of stepping back on Vermont soil. Somehow, despite the fear that coiled inside him for his father, as Kieran looked out over the vista, he felt a sudden peace slide over him. As weary as he was, the calm brought him near to tears.

"So tell me," he said simply after he pulled the car door closed behind him. Hayley buckled up then stiffened her arms against the steering wheel. Her eyes closed. He waited patiently.

"I don't know where to start. I guess when Brad—when we…" Her voice faltered, and she tilted her head to look at her brother. "It wasn't the same after the funeral." Unspoken was the residual disappointment she felt over Kieran's decision to return to England not six days after their brother's casket had been lowered into the ground. They had talked about it before, argued about it, shouted even as she'd lashed out in her temper and called him some

21

horrible names.

But how could Kieran have ever begun to defend himself when his sister could never know the real reason he had run? What did he say? There was an unspoken sorry there, and it tasted bitterly of grief and apology.

"How did it... What happened?"

"Truth is, Dad being ill was the least of our worries at the time. I mean he's a fighter, and he was going to win. Thing is...last month..."

Kieran felt his stomach drop knowing that what he was going to hear now was going to make him feel even smaller than he normally did where his family was concerned. He shouldn't feel so scared. He needed to know, and a flicker of anger snicked to life inside him. He should have known anyway. Someone should have phoned him, and he would have come home for a few weeks to help.

"Last month, he got a virus, and the treatment he had lowered his immunity, and it's not good. He's been sent back home and is on a drug regime, but he's so frail."

"Have they sent him home to die, Hays?" Kieran was terrified to ask, but he needed to know everything, if he was to be able to help.

"They just said he would be more comfortable at home." Kieran nodded. Professionals were not keen on giving out limits on people's lives, no one wanting to be open to legal repercussions for misdiagnosis. "He wouldn't let me tell you," she finished quietly.

"I don't understand. Why did no one...? Surely I had a right to know?"

"For the record, I didn't agree, but he didn't want you rushing back all gung ho, just because he was ill. He's always talking about his son the architect. He was, is, so proud of you, Kieran." Hayley's voice faltered, and Kieran heard sadness in her voice at the way she explained how their dad felt. He was so sorry for the way he had left, for the distance between him and his father.

"I should have been here, should have come home earlier."

22

He berated himself quietly, his tone certain, not looking to his sister for excuses for his behaviour. He should have put aside the guilt and the self-hatred and made himself the support of his family, the strong one.

"You didn't want to be at home. We knew that. You had a life in London."

"Hays, I'm sorry," he said carefully. How often had he said that in the past? He had never had the guts to talk to his sister about something so excruciating, had never given the real reasons why he had run so very far. Hayley just looked resigned, sad, thoughtful.

"I should have called you earlier, I know, but he made me promise. Can you see that?" Kieran heard the pleading in his sister's voice and was thrown that it was *she* who felt guilty. He was so used to feeling like he'd let his family down that realising she might have her own reactions confused and dismayed him. When had he become so self-centred? When had he stopped listening?

"Of course I understand." How could he begin to judge his sister for listening to what their dad had wanted her to do?

"Then there was the accident. Jordan..."

"Go on." Kieran cupped her face with his hands, seeing tears in her eyes, and trying not to reveal that the mention of that one name made him startle and cringe inside.

"He's been working so hard, trying to keep the company going. He was on site by himself..." Her voice tailed off as she closed her eyes. "If it wasn't for his cell dialling out..."

Kieran ignored the words. They didn't make sense to him, but he wasn't going to ask. There was some kind of bigger picture here. Why had Jordan been working alone? Where had the team of joiners and builders that worked for the company been?

"When Ben found him, he had cut his hand open on some kind of saw and lost so much blood." She opened her eyes and raised her gaze to his. "He nearly died, and I didn't know what else to do. With Dad...Jordan... I needed you here."

Carefully he raised a hand, and he knew instinctively what to say.

"It's okay, Hays, you did the right thing. You're a good daughter and an amazing sister." She pressed her cheek against his left hand, tears freely running down her face, her lower lip caught between her teeth, and Kieran just did what every big brother would do in this situation. Gently he pulled her into a cocoon of a hug. She was so small compared to him, trembling and hiccupping as she cried, and he locked his arms as carefully as he could about her.

"Everything will be okay," he whispered into her long blonde hair. "I'm here now. I want to help so tell me what I need to do."

Chapter Three

Jordan was irritable and tired, and his hand throbbed like a bitch. The stitches were itchy, and the sling he was forced to wear for at least another day both pulled at his neck and chafed him.

Sure, only a little over a week had passed since his run-in with the saw, but he wasn't healing quickly enough. The surgeon who had repaired the injury had muttered something about possible complications as a result of Jordan's physical condition and had been point-blank about the certainty of a slow recovery, due to his complete exhaustion.

However, once the first three days had passed without anything worse than having a hand that throbbed like a bitch, Jordan felt increasingly imprisoned and unable to break free.

He wasn't getting better fast enough. Ben had finished off the details, the restoration of Mistral House was completed, and the check had been deposited. And now he was useless.

The company had no big projects lined up to begin, nothing that would earn them anything in the way of a solid pay cheque. The Mistrals had volunteered to write a testimonial, and indeed to speak with prospective customers.

But he was still so freaking exhausted, sleeping and eating, driven by determination to recover. Jordan hated feeling so helpless. Even the small jobs they'd had at the time of his accident, from the Willis' porch to the Magsers' bathroom, lay outside of his capability until the bandages came off. Not being able to work, worrying about cash flow and being in pain was not a good combination on the best of days. Today, with a meeting at the bank in three hours, he was the proverbial bear sporting a sore paw.

He made his way to the main house and found Anna preparing breakfast. She seemed to be preparing a lot of food considering it was only him there. Phil had got out of hospital but he still wasn't eating properly.

"Where's Phil?"

"In his office. Hiding I think," Anna said.

"How's he doing?" Jordan asked carefully. Anna looked pale and tired.

"He's doing okay. But he's in pain."

"Where's Hayley?" he asked.

"She slept out last night," Anna said as she spooned eggs onto a plate for him.

"Where did she say she was going?" Jordan asked again. He slipped into the much used role of big brother as easily as pulling on his jeans in the morning. After all, he damn near *was* her big brother, especially with Brad gone and Kieran on another continent. He had a right and a reason to be worried. As soon as Anna told him that Hayley hadn't been home, he started fretting even though he knew he had to accept that the girl he thought of as five with pigtails had actually reached adulthood and had even had sex. He didn't want to think about that in too much detail. Realising that Hayley had grown up meant looking at what he'd been doing while she had. And remembering the past proved just so difficult to do.

"She's twenty-two, sweetie. If she wants to stay out, that's her choice. Maybe she was with that nice young man Alex."

Anna sounded so accommodating, as if it didn't worry her that her youngest child was out God knows where with God knows who. Alex might seem like a good guy, and Jordan had even grudgingly admitted he appeared to be a solid stable influence on the normally flighty Hayley, but still... He knew exactly what was in the head of a twenty-five-year-old man. After all, he was only twenty-nine himself, and he had a good memory. Resentment built inside him, sudden and bitter. After Brad, they should have been more careful with knowing where their kids were and what they were doing.

Shit. Where had that thought come from? Brad had been a grown man. What had happened to him had nothing to do with Anna and Phil. They were good parents, and they had made a good family. It also wasn't their fault Kieran was gone. He ruthlessly pushed down the irrational imaginings to where they belonged, way down where he stored his own guilt.

"Should've told us," Jordan snapped in return, anger fighting with fear in his gut. She was so little, even at twenty-two, slim and petite and so blindly trusting of everything and everyone around her.

"Jordan..." Anna turned from the skillet, wiping her hands on her apron and looking at him with that patented mother expression that she did so well. It never failed to calm him down. "She texted to say she was okay. That is as much as we are going to get. We know she's okay – she said so."

Jordan grimaced. Recently all he seemed to be able do was focus on the shit that was happening, or on the worst that *could* happen. It was so easy to let a million thoughts race through his mind, every one coloured with death and blood and fear. He could imagine a kidnapper taking the phone and texting as her, or her being coerced... Jesus, it didn't bear thinking about.

"I'm going to be having words with her," he grumped, concentrating on the plate of food that Anna placed in front of him. He wasn't even hungry, anxiety nibbling away at him until his stomach was one big knotted mass. Patiently, and fully aware that Anna was watching him as she had done ever since his accident, he forked eggs and bacon into his mouth, the taste of them like ashes.

Eating didn't stop him from brooding, and being watched didn't stop his mood from spiralling lower. If anything, the combination of the two made everything worse. The three o'clock appointment at the bank was still looming and he was worried about what they would say.

Jordan had to go on his own, Phil wasn't well enough to be there with him, but he was determined that he would be involved in dealing with the finances for the company. He wanted to be hands-on, it was his company and on and on. Whenever Phil started talking that way, Jordan just listened as patiently as he could, trying not to feel too hurt that Phil was determined to hold on so tightly. After all, hadn't he been running the company just fine for the last two years?

When the kitchen door opened, and Hayley took a step into the battleground, Jordan was on her like a ton of bricks, launching to his feet with temper running through him like fire.

"Where the hell have you been? We've been damn scared you were in a ditch or something. For God's sake, your momma was worried." Jordan's voice was loud and quick and his temper on a rare high. He saw Hayley look at her mom with raised eyebrows, receiving a small smile and a shrug of delicate shoulders in return. She wasn't taking him seriously. God damn it, she needed to take him seriously.

"Jordan—" Hayley started quickly, but he interrupted before she could get any words out. He took a step towards her, his free hand gripping her arm.

"You should have let us know where you were."

"I—"

"Just so I don't go ripping up the area looking for you." He realised he was shaking her, unaware of anything else, his temper making his actions sharp, until a hand rested on his arm.

"She was with me." A low voice was in his ear, lost in the sound of a gasp from Anna then complete and utter silence for a second as a tableau of shocked, frozen people engraved itself on Jordan's mind.

It was Anna who broke the awkward silence, launching herself at the son she hadn't seen in too long. Jordan's softly spoken "Kieran" was drowned out by the squeal from Anna, and the rush of hugs and welcomes and the refrains of *why didn't you tell me*? Everyone talked over each other with laughter and jokes.

Typical. After all this time, Kieran freaking Addison walks through the door, and suddenly everyone conveniently forgets how he ran out and left them all.

Jordan stared at the man who had just shaken his world to the roots. He struggled to see the boy who had left only days after that rainy Tuesday when they had buried Brad. This Kieran was different — not a boy, but a man. Gone were the uncoordinated lankiness of youth and the floppy blond bangs that were forever determined to cover his grey eyes. Instead here was a man in control — tall, strong, with styled, shorter hair…and a gaze that wouldn't meet Jordan's. When it came down to it, Jordan felt the shock driving into him that Kieran Addison had deigned to return to the Addison fold at all. He waited, watching Anna welcome home the prodigal son, allowing the moments of reconnection. Then he said the first thing that came to his mind as he looked at Kieran and cursed his arrival for so many reasons he couldn't begin to list them.

"What the hell are you doing here?"

"I've come home," Kieran said carefully, steeling himself to look at the man he had run from twice. When he did finally look, he felt nothing but shock. He remembered Jordan laughing with Brad, crying at Brad's funeral. He didn't recall ever before seeing the hate and despair that was in Jordan's tired green eyes. He was smartly dressed in a dark green button-down shirt and khaki pants, his dark hair neat and short as it had always been. He'd shaved, if the small pearl of dried blood near his upper lip was anything to go by. Somehow, though, he seemed to occupy a smaller space than the Jordan of Kieran's memory. He was thinner, and the overall set of his shoulders showed incredible exhaustion. Still beautiful, but diminished in strength and determination, as if he'd poured all of himself out into something else.

"Why?" Jordan certainly wasn't pulling punches. Kieran reared back a little, a spark of anger battling with jet lag and shock.

"I asked him to," Hayley intervened quickly, drawing Jordan's attention away from Kieran. Kieran looked from her to his mom, attempting to telegraph his need for space, for time before he was ready to deal with everyone's questions.

"Would you like breakfast, honey?" His mom was hovering, clearly looking for something to change the subject, and she'd hit the nail on the head. It really had been a long time since he had eaten his momma's cooking. And he did want to sit and eat his fill of one of her breakfasts.

But something else held first priority. Pointedly ignoring Jordan, who was opening his mouth to continue his inquisition, Kieran answered his mom with a query of his own.

"Mom, where's Dad? I need to see him," he said softly, "then I need you to tell me everything." His mom raised a hand to her mouth, and he noticed the fine tremble in it and the lines around her eyes. She had aged since he'd left, and he couldn't help wondering what he'd missed in the years he had been away from home. He had last seen her at the funeral, watching her closely as the casket had been lowered into the ground. She had been strong then, the glue that held the family together as they grieved. Now though, in the two years since Brad had died, she had lost weight, seemed thinner, her face lined with worry and age and she appeared nervous and on edge. He remembered little else from the funeral. The visit had been one big blur of grief and shame. True, it had been two years ago, but he didn't recall his mom looking quite so small and frail. He still retained images of her as the strong homemaker, the backbone of their family, and it overwhelmed him just how much she'd had to bear, losing one son to wanderlust and another to death. That had been bad enough, but then with her husband, her rock, falling ill...

"He's in the study," she said softly, her eyes filling with tears.

"Kieran—" The tone in Jordan's voice held warning and accusation, but Kieran hushed him sharply with a sharp shake of his head. Then, very gently, he pulled his mom into a tight embrace.

"Momma," he whispered for only her to hear, then eased back, feeling his throat thicken with emotion, his breath tighten in his chest. Closing her eyes briefly, she smiled, her lips tremulous and uncertain. When she opened them again, she reached up to touch his face. She traced across his cheekbone and brushed his lips with her cold fingertips, finally resting her hand flat on his chest.

"Your dad'll never say it, but he needs all of his family here."

Kieran took the familiar route, past the fridge covered with magnets and notes, and into the hallway. He stopped just out of sight of everyone, took a moment to compose himself, then opened the door to the study.

Chapter Four

The ride to the bank was uncomfortable. Kieran sprawled against his side of the cab of the ancient GMC C1500 pickup, yawning. Jordan sat ramrod stiff, tight-lipped, his good hand clutching the wheel. They hadn't spoken much after Kieran had disappeared into his dad's study for a good half an hour.

When Kieran and his dad had emerged from what Anna lovingly called Phil's Pit, both men had been red-eyed. Even then, Jordan hadn't been able to find anything inside that remotely resembled pity. He knew his heart was hard, knew it was out of character, but all he could feel for Kieran was resentment and distrust. Why the hell had he come home now? Why pick this very moment to fall back into Jordan's life, just as working hard had started to heal some of the grief. He didn't need Kieran here, didn't want Kieran here. No one needed Kieran here, not if they all really thought about it. Hayley had Jordan, and damn it, Jordan was doing a fine job of being a big brother. As for Phil and Anna, they didn't need Kieran back. All he would bring with him were his wandering ways and his childish view of what was real.

He shouldn't be here, sitting in Jordan's truck watching the scenery roll by outside, his stare bored. Brad should be here. His Brad—Jordan's lover—Jordan's other half. It should be Brad sitting next to Jordan—laughing with him, loving him—not Kieran. The bitterness inside Jordan stopped him from displaying the most basic good manners, let alone conversation. His hand ached, and a headache pounded up from his clenched jaw. *Get the bank visit over and done. Stay focused.* Jordan wanted it finished, sorted, so that Kieran could realise again how much he didn't need to be here. He could go back to London where he was out of Jordan's sight and out of his thoughts.

In silence they had driven, and in silence they sat opposite the assistant bank manager, David Mitchell. The man, who had graduated high school two years before Jordan, made the usual fuss, the welcomes and said, "Are you here for a visit?"

Kieran answered everything calmly—his accent a variation of what it had been all the years before he'd left. Not quite so easy or drawled, it was more clipped and precise. Probably due to living in London for years, Jordan guessed. He narrowed his eyes as he watched the exchange between David and the returning son. He didn't have any time for David either. The asshole kept hitting on him, backing him into corners and suggesting that Jordan might like a taste of what David could give him. David had been obnoxious in school, and he was just as obnoxious now—a rotund, superior idiot who really thought entirely too much of himself.

"I must say I expected your father to join us here today," David said, not looking at Jordan and instead directing his half-question, half-statement directly to Kieran. Jordan refused to rise to the bait, accustomed to David and his obnoxious one-upmanship after many meetings regarding the company finances for Addison Construction.

"He thought it would be good for me to be hands-on," Jordan heard Kieran say, and he felt temper churning in his stomach at those simple words. Phil had stood in the kitchen, his hand on Kieran's arm, a grin as bright as day on his face and had announced that Kieran had agreed to take over the running of the company.

Hurt had knifed through Jordan as immediate as breath. They didn't need Kieran. Brad had died, left Jordan on his own, and he had been running everything just fine. He may not be blood-related to the Addisons, but shit, he had sweated more than blood to keep everything going.

What the hell did Phil think Wonder Boy was going to do anyway? The company was fucked. There were the two quotes for architect-driven builds. Jordan held the deep hope that something might come of them. Other than the two small jobs for next week, and those two quotes, they had jack shit.

"Well, as you know, the bank has every faith in the Addisons," David began. To Jordan's ears, his voice slithered, oily and insincere. He rifled through some papers and pressed keys on a calculator, a frown on his face as he looked up and glanced first at Jordan then at Kieran. "Your debt profile is looking quite healthy. The check you deposited today, all being well, should clear the outstanding monies owed the bank, and leave you with a credit of some four thousand dollars."

Jordan sat back in his chair, relief washing over him as he calculated project work and salary against expected work. If he didn't take a salary again this month and next, then Addison Construction could probably guarantee at least two months of good running time. He chanced a quick glance at Kieran, who was leafing through his own paper copies, seemingly unconcerned as to what David was saying. Clearly Kieran had no freaking idea about debt profiles. Jordan was intimately aware of the threatening meaning behind those two words. He'd been dealing with their implications for going on two years.

"I just have the issue of the missed mortgage payments." Silence.

Jordan blinked, the words mortgage suddenly searing into his brain. *What mortgage?*

"Okay," Kieran said simply, obviously unaware the bottom had just fallen out of Jordan's world. "Can you give me an idea of what is needed here, a whole picture of the company so I can get a grip on it?"

"Of course," David said politely. As he was talking, he was looking directly at Jordan, a small quirk of a smile on his face that only Jordan would recognise.

Jordan listened as David itemised each transaction, and the meeting he'd had with Phil a few years back listing the Addison house as surety against a loan.

"What loan? Why would Phil take out a loan?" Jordan asked confused, suddenly feeling like the world was spinning way too damn fast.

"I'm sorry, Mr Salter, I'm not at liberty to say," David said.

Jordan wanted to knock that smarmy look from his face as David casually closed the file in front of him.

"Not at liberty?" Jordan snapped abruptly. He knew the company inside out. For all intents and purposes, he co-managed the company with Phil. Why all of a sudden was he not privy to important information?

"Until I have power of attorney signed over from Mr Addison" — he nodded at Kieran — "Senior, I'm unable to release any information on the particulars of why a debt was accrued."

Jordan couldn't believe what he was hearing. They were unable to release information to Phil's son? What the fuck was going on here? Kieran, for his part, seemed mainly unconcerned, but Jordan could admit he wasn't totally surprised there. Why would Kieran choose today to actually give a freaking damn about his family or their business? And what loan? Jordan had never been told about any damn loan. He'd been working every second to keep this company afloat, and Phil had taken out a loan behind his back? He couldn't get his head around this, floundering at his lack of knowledge, at being kept in the dark. He realised he was in some kind of semi-shock and wondered how this could get any worse.

"How much to clear the outstanding mortgage payments? I'm more than certain that you can advise me of the total figure," Kieran said crisply. Jordan glanced over at the calmly impassive man who was scribbling notes on the back of one of many papers. Kieran's voice was ice — cold and hard and business-like, no passion there at all.

David rechecked figures, tapping at the calculator and sighing with great physical exaggeration. "Without touching the four thousand in the personal account" — he paused, lifting his gaze to focus on Kieran — "we would need somewhere in the region of sixteen thousand dollars to clear the debt today. Paying today would stop us having to pursue for the entire balance."

Shit. Jordan sat back in his chair. How had Phil got so far behind on a loan that Jordan didn't even know about? What the fuck were they going to do now? There was no way Jordan had access to any kind of work that would clear sixteen thousand dollars immediately. And was it just Jordan's imagination or did David sound smug, like he was waiting for Kieran to fold, to give up, and for the errant son to admit defeat before he had even started?

How the hell could the bank expect any party at this table to come up with sixteen thousand dollars just like that? Jordan added David's smugness to the list of things that made him squirm whenever he was in the same room as him.

"I will organise payment for you today," Kieran finally said confidently, and Jordan frowned.

Last he'd heard, Kieran was working hard for nothing and struggling to find airfare home to visit his family, for whatever reason he might have been needed. How did he expect to clear sixteen thousand dollars in debt at the drop of a hat? If he could, then Kieran obviously had money that even his struggling family knew nothing about, and that only deepened Jordan's shock-fuelled temper. He remembered the times he had found Kieran's mom in the kitchen in tears after a phone conversation with her middle child, offering hugs and quiet support. *He's working hard, doesn't have the money to come home. He's making a name for himself. It isn't his fault.* It was a mantra that she'd focused on, and one that even Jordan had started to believe.

"Payment of the outstanding amount in full?" David asked with clear disbelief in his voice. Jordan narrowed his eyes at the tone. David's nose was evidently more than just a little put out of joint by Addison Junior sitting at the desk and clearing problems from the table. "Future debt—"

"Will be dealt with," Kieran interrupted quickly and firmly. "I need access to a computer to transfer funds, and your recommendation, perhaps a list of five names, for a local lawyer to draw up a power of attorney."

David blustered a little. Kieran had obviously covered every base, and it clearly wasn't what the pudgy bank assistant manager had been expecting. Finally the weaselly ass showed Kieran to the next room and a computer that he could use. Kieran stood, shook hands with David and gestured for Jordan to leave. Stubborn pride made Jordan stand where he was, halfway between the assistant manager's office and the private room with the computer. He was torn. He wanted to punch David until the man lay in an unconscious heap on the floor, but he also wanted to punch Kieran just as damn hard. Temper was roiling inside him, hot and heavy in his stomach, and he clenched his fists. He hated being out of control, hated that he was out of the loop. He didn't deserve this, and he had to do something. Anything.

"I'll meet you at the car," Kieran said bluntly, twisting a hand into Jordan's jacket sleeve and subtly pulling him away from David.

Jordan snatched his arm back. No fucking way was he being sent out of this bank like some kind of recalcitrant child.

"I'll be fifteen minutes," Kieran added, irritation threading his voice. Jordan opened his mouth to say something, but found that temper had short-circuited his brain, and he could think of nothing to say that would make sense. Kieran's eyes glittered with an emotion that Jordan couldn't understand, then with a small shake of his head and lips pressed hard into a tight line, he took the step into the computer room. Shutting the door in Jordan's face sent a very clear message.

As soon as the door had shut, David turned on him with intent.

"I could make this all go away," David said under his breath, leaning into Jordan in the tight space that led from his office to the lobby. Jordan flinched. David was five inches shorter and about thirty pounds heavier than he was. Jordan could smack him down in an instant, so why did the man intimidate him? David ran a finger down Jordan's arm from shoulder to wrist, a lascivious expression making Jordan's stomach heave.

"The offer is still there. All you need to do, Salter, is bend your pretty self over that desk for me, and I can make sure all this stress is avoided."

Jordan stood there for seconds, aware only that Kieran had closed the door and that David was propositioning him again. It was too much, too hot in this damn bank, and the futility of his anger pushed him to move. Easing David away, he strode out of the dark corridor and through the main banking lobby, until he finally stood in the sunshine and could breathe fresh air.

Fuck David, and fuck Kieran.

Chapter Five

Kieran leant back against the closed door, his head physically throbbing with everything he had just learnt. He realised he was holding his breath, waiting for Jordan to storm in. He knew the man must have so many questions, but he also knew that he couldn't deal with him yet.

Seeing Jordan again was too much too soon. Kieran sensed the unspoken anger in him. Damn it, it wasn't like he was even trying to hide it. Jordan looked so different from Kieran's memories of him. He looked gaunt, tired, ill — older than his years, and so damned angry.

At the moment, though, his memories and his perceptions were snarled in knots complicated by grief and shock that had grown into a Medusa's head of overwhelming horror. Just attempting to understand everything threatened to take him to his knees.

When his dad had said he'd been forced to mortgage the house to get a cash injection just to keep the company going, Kieran hadn't even needed to ask why. He knew why. The family company had always been Brad's legacy. His brother had been the one who excelled at hands-on construction and renovation. Kieran's strength had lain in design, in seeing the way things *could* be.

His dad clearly had been desperate to hold on to the last thing that kept Brad's memory alive every day. Kieran had difficulty comprehending how far his dad had actually gone *to* keep that dream. Over one hundred thousand dollars. *Shit.*

He crossed to the computer and collapsed into the chair, staring down dazedly when he felt his knees still shaking.

For a short time, he huddled, resting his face in his hands, half waiting for the door to smack open and crash against the wall. *Stay away, Jordan. Stay away,* part of his mind pleaded. *No, I need you,* the other part whispered.

When it became clear that Jordan had decided not to follow him in, he began to think more rationally. He needed to start pulling his thoughts together in order to clear the debt. He logged on to his accounts and transferred his meagre savings into his checking account. It was the codes for the final account where he hesitated—his 'away from Jordan, away from memories, away from pain' freedom account. It was like the pain was in him again, the knife of agony in his back, and he shifted uncomfortably in the seat. He had vowed not to touch this money for himself. He didn't even consider it to be truly his, and he felt like a cheat. Still, if this wasn't an emergency, he didn't know what was. The money would do some good now.

He input his password, hesitating only briefly, then, with acceptance of what he needed to do, he clicked on the transfer button, hoping to hell the exchange rate was good enough that the money would clear all the debt. He waited for the calculated amount, glancing at the company account number for Addison Construction handed to him by the arrogant smug dick in the suit. Finally the amount tallied on the screen. Seventeen thousand two hundred thirty-four dollars and twenty-one cents. Kieran released his pent-up sigh of relief. It was enough with a small bit to spare. Without hesitation, he input the bank's details, and with the proviso that it would take four working days, the transaction was complete, leaving just over one thousand dollars to Kieran's name.

He closed the screen, wobbled to his feet and stiffened his knees until he could stride across the room and open the door. He had heard muffled talking in the hallway and he really hoped that the assistant manager had moved on.

He wasn't the least bit surprised to find the guy hovering outside. "Four working days. We'll be in touch," was all

Kieran said. After a cool, measuring look that would leave David with no doubts about Kieran's opinion of him, he stalked out of the bank.

Half of him wanted to see Jordan, and the other half demanded he ran fast and far away. Stepping out onto the dusty, busy street, he scanned for sight of the man in his thoughts, finally spotting him leaning against the wall of the deli, his right foot flat against the wall and his head bowed in thought.

Whatever it was—the attitude, the temper Kieran knew Jordan held in check or maybe the sadness in his beautiful green eyes—Kieran felt himself falling all over again for the man who had made him run. The need for Brad's lover was still so strong inside him.

He ignored the sounds of the street, an immoveable object to the few people who walked around him. He cursed the day that he had seen Jordan Robert Salter as someone to want. That had destroyed everything.

Jordan spotted him and pushed away from the deli, moving swiftly to his truck and starting the engine, clearly waiting for Kieran to get in. For a moment Kieran considered walking back home, but living six miles outside of Cooper's Bay meant he'd have one hell of a walk on thirty-six hours of no sleep. It wouldn't do him any good to be even more tired than he was already, and it certainly wouldn't help him deal with his new responsibilities.

The ride back to the house began in silence, Kieran lost in his own thoughts. He wasn't stupid. He realised he was in mild shock, lost in focusing on the realisation that yet again he was penniless.

He had promised himself when he'd started his junior position at Drewitt-Nate, that he would save his money and repay every penny of the debt he had. Save and clear it without asking his family for help, proving that he was a man and not some selfish boy who had run away to hide. Hoarding money in his savings account, he had watched the balance grow. That same balance had hit zero momentarily when he'd finally paid back what he'd owed in tuition fees. But, filled with intense pride at his achievement, the near-zero balance hadn't fazed him.

He had relied on the fact that Evan paid fifty per cent of the rent on their crappy apartment just off the main high street. It wasn't the best of places, but it was their own. Kieran had made a life for himself and had even got himself a boyfriend. The relationship had been short-lived with a volatile ending when he'd found said boyfriend in bed with another man.

Returning home one day as a full-fledged architect, a man with letters after his name, a man who had done something with his life, had always been his goal. Instead, sitting here next to the very person that had caused him to run, he felt like a small child. It hurt.

The pounding in his head hadn't lessened. Indeed, it had been joined by the razor sharp agony of an impending migraine. He closed his eyes, leaning his hot forehead against the cool window of the worn, rusted truck. All he felt inside was confusion. Why had no one asked him to come home earlier? Were they afraid of him, disgusted with his leaving in the first place? Did they blame him for some of it? Why had his dad never told him just how much financial trouble he was in? Why had he re-mortgaged the house? Even Jordan hadn't known about that one, that much had been clear.

Kieran's emails to his mom and dad and their replies had always been filled with the inane chatter of a family for whom tragedy still lurked too near, still burned too hot and bright for discussion. Their silence had nearly ripped them apart.

He guessed he was as guilty as they were for holding things in, for not telling the whole story. Not one of them had known about the building site accident, or the small amount of compensation he had received, or the real reasons why he never came home for Christmas. But, Kieran realised as he looked back, his dad had guessed at least some of it.

"Why are you really leaving, son?" his dad had asked sadly when Kieran had left for college. He'd stood at the departure gate, uncertainty etched into his features.

Kieran had given his usual answer. "It's an adventure, Dad. It's a good school, and it's me 'n Evan against the world." He'd always finished that particular lie with a smile, a smile that his dad had returned before grabbing him for a bone-crushing final hug goodbye. The money left to him in his Nana's will had been enough for the flight, a deposit on the crappy rooms he would share with Evan, and to make it an easier decision to just pack his bags and go.

Distance had provided perspective, and the memories of what had made him leave seemed to dim and become almost non-existent. He grew up and put his feelings for his brother's boyfriend into perspective, deciding they were just a childhood infatuation, nothing more. He'd become an adult.

"Why did you leave so quickly?" Jordan's voice cut through Kieran's mental rehashing sharp and clean, jerking him back to the here and now with startling force.

"Leave?" Kieran used the best delaying tactic he had, throwing the question right back at Jordan.

"After Brad's... After the funeral, you only stayed for a few days then you just went. Why?"

Kieran didn't have an answer for that one. Well, not one he could share with the class. "I had to leave. It was all too much," he hedged, hoping Jordan was going to leave this one alone.

"Bullshit," Jordan replied quickly. "Your momma needed you, your dad, Hays... And you just up and left without even a goodbye."

"They understood. I had a new job, and I needed to go back to London."

"No, Kieran, you needed to be *here*. For *them*."

Kieran felt anger start to build in the pit of his stomach.

Was Jordan being deliberately obtuse? Did he not remember the funeral as clearly as Kieran did, when only days later the need for physical comfort turned from a hug and whispered words of grief to a kiss? A kiss with his brother's boyfriend in his own family's back yard? When his love for Jordan had spilled over common decency?

"What about what I needed?" Kieran snapped, finally tired of whatever Jordan was trying to say. He could skirt the issue of the kiss forever. He wasn't going to be the one to bring it up if Jordan didn't, and the best place to hide sorrow and regret was to bury it deep in anger.

"What you needed was to grow up and be there for your family," Jordan replied, giving no quarter in his perspective of the situation. Apparently he'd decided that the time was right for not withholding anything.

Kieran stiffened his spine and moved away from his huddled position against the truck door, half turning to Jordan. He couldn't believe what he had just heard. Jordan was telling *him* to grow up?

"I wasn't some stupid kid, Jordan, and what about you? Kissing your dead lover's brother only days after he was buried? Don't you think you fucked it up enough for both of us?"

Jordan turned the wheel so hard that Kieran made solid contact with the door. The older man pulled onto the shoulder of the long, dusty side road and cut the engine. He yanked the keys from the ignition and wrenched open his door. His silence shouting words he couldn't express, he stomped over to the shade of a spreading ancient oak tree and stood there, fists bunched, face white with rage and grief.

Kieran sighed. He should never have broken the fragile and unspoken truce between them. He didn't want to remember that day any more than Jordan did. He undid his seat belt and climbed down from the cab. Kieran was sure that, for Jordan, it had been grief that had sought physical comfort. Kieran and Brad had been so similar in build and

44

even looks. Kieran knew why the kiss had happened—it was a last desperate grab by Jordan for some memory of Brad. That was all it had signified.

"You come back here, Kieran..." Jordan started, his gaze spitting fire, tension bracketing his mouth and eyes, anger carved into his face. "We don't need you. We are working fine without you. Why don't you just fuck off back to London?"

"Yeah, sure, everything's really goin' great, isn't it?" Kieran snapped back, aware he was only adding fuel to Jordan's temper. "Going so well my dad had to mortgage his God damned house."

"You fucking son of a bitch." Jordan lunged so fast Kieran didn't register the move until he had backpedalled under the force of Jordan's assault and was pinned against the metal of the truck. Jordan's snarling face was mere inches from him. He tried to push him away. It should have been easy given Jordan had a bandaged arm in a sling, but Jordan angled his body to protect his vulnerable limb, temper giving strength to his stance.

"Let me go," Kieran said as calmly as he could. *Easy, Kieran, no panic, slow down,* he thought, trying to talk himself out of the rising panic attack that was a residual gift of the accident.

"Let you go? Do you have any fucking idea what your family has been through? That we scrape from one job to another, that your momma has a second job to keep us above water? Did you know Hays decided against going to freaking MIT to study math and instead goes to the local community college? She used her nana's money to buy materials for the last job. Did you know that?"

"Jordan—"

"Yet here you are, the freaking prodigal son, returned from London doing whatever the fuck you were doing, throwing money around like water, like it's nothing, coming back to save your family. Some kind of damn cavalry."

"I—"

45

"Do you know the hours I put in for the company? All to keep us in the black."

Kieran glanced at Jordan's bandaged hand. It must be painful, all clenched and screwed up into Kieran's shirt. Kieran hadn't known what Jordan had been doing for his family, because no one had told him what had been happening. Every letter, every text, every email, all full of lies. Hays had said she wanted vocational work, that college was not on her to-do list, and Kieran hadn't even questioned that.

"I'm back now," Kieran said, trying to pull himself away from Jordan's grasp, but that served only to twist the material even more solidly in Jordan's fist. "Thank you for what you've done, but I'm home. This is my family, and I will sort it from now on."

"*Your* family?" Jordan's voice was deceptively calm. "Yours?" he repeated, this time somewhat more of a question than the last. Kieran was confused. *Yes*. His family.

"Years, Kieran. For years I have kept this company alive, held your momma when she cried, supported your dad through his tests and worked on my own for the last year. I even punched out Louis Matthews when he pushed it too far with Hayley. Fuck, Kieran. I'm nearly fucking thirty, and I don't know where my twenties went. Where were you? And who the fuck do you think you are to come back here like you finally give a shit?"

That there. That accusation hurt. Kieran pushed him away in one collection of bunched muscles and strength, watching as Jordan stumbled back from Kieran although his temper kept him upright.

"What is it, Jordan?" Sudden compassion welled inside Kieran. Jordan had been a motherless friend of Brad's whose dad was your typical deadbeat alcoholic father, and he'd been cared for mostly by the neighbours. And since the day Jordan had first come to dinner at the age of eight Jordan had been part of the Addison family. "Is it that you think you are going to be pushed to one side?"

"*My* family, Kieran, not yours. You don't deserve them! But I see them welcome you home with open arms like I'm not even there."

"Jordan..." Kieran took a step towards him, something inside him pushing to comfort, but Jordan just stepped away.

"Blood—" Jordan started, but stopped, clenching his fists at his side. Kieran knew what he was going to say—'*Blood is thicker than water*'—and he wanted to head that thought off at the pass.

"J..." he began, barely aware he had slipped into using the nickname he had used for Jordan before everything had gone wrong. "You are, always have been, part of this family. You and Brad were like this married couple when you were twenty. You know my family loves you. I would never do or say anything to try to change that."

"Fuck you, Kieran. Just—fuck you." The subject clearly over, Jordan clambered back into the truck. Kieran followed, although the air remained thick with tension and resentment. Kieran didn't know what to say so he chose the best road he could see and said nothing. He had his own problems to think about without adding the huge chip from Jordan's shoulder to the pile. Jordan may have been Brad's boyfriend, and he may have worked for Addison Construction since he had left college, but it still didn't give him the right to judge Kieran for wanting to come back to his family. Didn't Jordan realise how hard it was for Kieran to even be in the same vehicle with Jordan, let alone talk to him?

They reached the edge of the town and the sprawling new houses that he knew his family had been involved in building. Suddenly everything piled up inside him and pushed him to get out of the truck.

"Stop the truck," he demanded, moving his hand to unlock the belt. Jordan snapped his head around, the question clear on his face. He didn't react fast enough for Kieran, who fumbled with the buckle and pulled the belt off. "Stop the fucking truck," he repeated.

"Shit, Kieran, what the fuck?" Jordan pulled the truck off to the shoulder, a dusty dead grass edge, a litany of curses on his lips.

Kieran climbed out from the cab before the truck had even properly stopped moving. He felt a spasm in his back and knew he should get back into the truck, but there was no way he was going to do that.

"What the hell?" Jordan snapped, but Kieran ignored him.

"I'll make my own way home from here," he said simply. He strode off into the trees to one side, only relaxing when he heard the engine start and Jordan pulling away, his obvious frustration echoed in the way he floored the accelerator and left, the truck's tires squealing.

Kieran walked for some time, feeling tension tight across his shoulders as he went over in detail the accusations that Jordan had thrown at him. That he hadn't cared, that he had let his family down. He knew the latter was true. He had let the family down, disappointed his dad and betrayed his own brother for God's sake. He rounded the bend of the park, the new housing area behind him, the older houses from the original town in front of him, then he stopped.

Everything was so different here, especially compared to London. Where London was chaos and bustle and the history of centuries, Cooper's Bay could only claim two hundred years of written history. It had been settled back when dirt roads served only the town and a few nearby homesteads and travellers used the river to transport themselves and their goods to areas not reachable in any other way. Cooper's Bay had developed a modest tourist trade during the late nineteenth and early twentieth centuries when the most adventurous of the very wealthy in New York and Boston had summered there.

Now it was dull with the dust of recession, some businesses shut down already, his family's own business hit so hard. Sighing, he crouched down then slumped against a tall tree, the shade cool and comforting. It was impossible to guarantee sunshine in England, and light and heat were never so intense that a person blinked and shortened his breath when he stepped outside. London, however, *did* have the rain that washed the architecture of a million inspired minds, that made carved stone and impressive palisades sparkle with the sheen of moisture.

It had been Kieran's favourite pastime, in jacket and boots, to traverse the back roads, the maze of interconnected streets, dodging puddles metres wide and touching each building with eager fingers as if he could take in the history of a place through his skin.

There was a coffee shop, nothing special, not a Starbucks or a Costa Coffee, but a simple mom-and-pop shop, and it offered a haven only two minutes' walk from the office.

Its lot carved out of a side road and buried in amongst the newer glass and stone of the twentieth century, the coffee shop had wide windows that looked out at nothing more than brick walls. It was there that he would sit and drink coffee, reading a paper or sketching, thoughtful as he did so. He had grown used to the sound of rain splashing down on those windows, tracing paths down the bricks.

Kieran was an artist. There was nothing more to be said. As an architect, he would always have the heart of an artist. Still, he saw art in the strangest of things. He had promised himself, listening to the sound of rain and tasting the bitter coffee, that one day he would be responsible for buildings that stood the test of time. Buildings that a student in the future would want to touch so that they could connect to the past.

He drew his knees up, squirming at the pain in his lower back, then sighing as the twinges faded when he shifted to the left. He was used to the tenderness, the result of a stupid accident. An early assignment with Drewitt-Nate to a building site in Canary Wharf had ended with him and two others injured under falling scaffolding. Kieran had been lucky, as had the two others, that they hadn't died that day. The other two had managed to scramble free and call for help. He'd been trapped under the rubble and the scaffolding, with the worst of the injuries and that had really *only* been a huge gash on his lower back and a broken femur. He had received just short of twenty thousand pounds in compensation as a result of the accident. It had been the start of his savings account, and now, what had been left of it was gone.

He sat under the tree for some time, so many memories and so many thoughts twisting without resolution. He had never phoned home about the accident, not even when the surgeons had suggested he might not walk again. There was no point.

He hadn't wanted anyone coming to London for him, and he'd had Evan. Evan had always been there for him. During his recovery and physical therapy, he had made excuses for not visiting home in emails, offering exams at first then work as reasons.

Stubborn pride, he wanted to believe, had made him study and live away from home. His dad had said he was stupid, that there were colleges in Vermont that could give Kieran what he wanted. The ensuing arguments had been huge, enormous, out of proportion. Horrible things had been said on both sides. Inexcusable things. Kieran had not wanted to go to work for Brad. He'd been adamant. He was going to make his own way, do his own thing, out of his brother's shadow, away from his brother's lover, although he would never have said that, no matter how angry he might become.

Jordan.

And it had all come full circle. Here he was, back in Cooper's Bay, back with his family, doing exactly what he'd said he wouldn't do. Only Brad wasn't here. Would never be here again.

Kieran needed to see him.

Decision made, he used the tree to steady him as he stood. His back ached and he rubbed it, although that didn't really help. Then he followed the paths he remembered until he finally reached the large iron gates — permanently open and enmeshed with vines and climbing flowers. It looked very pretty, very calm. Kieran stopped, blinked and tried to get his bearings, closing his eyes and imagining the days from before.

Two years ago, the sombre cortege had meandered slowly through the graveyard, and Kieran could see the grief and the sadness as clear as yesterday in his mind. Hays had been so young, and his mom and dad had been focusing on her in her grief. Jordan had stood so still next to the hole in the ground, wavering once, twice, then stilling himself and not moving again. The rest was a blur. Words had been spoken that were designed to comfort, but nothing could pull Kieran away from that grave until only he and Brad's love had remained, Kieran on one side of the open grave and Jordan on the other.

"Can you tell me how it happened? I mean I read the report and I spoke to the cop, but I don't understand," Kieran said, *his voice low, stunned as Jordan twisted his hands in his short hair, his face pale in grief and green eyes filled with tears.*

"He took his seat belt off," Jordan said, *his voice broken.*

"They said that, said he was drunk, that he had taken something as well." Jordan nodded, and Kieran saw red. *"Why did you let him do that?"* he snapped, *striding around the grave until he stood a mere measure from Jordan.*

Jordan shook his head, taking a step back and raising his hands. "I tried to get him to stop drinking, to put the belt on, Kieran. God knows I tried."

"Not hard enough."

"Shit." Jordan couldn't seem to string sentences together, and Kieran had a small amount of satisfaction in seeing Jordan cry.

"You could have stopped him," Kieran spat, *pushing at Jordan's chest, causing him to stumble back a step.*

"No. I couldn't. No one stops your brother — stopped your brother — from doing anything."

"Then why did he do it? What was so God damn important that he took drugs and got drunk? What were you doing to him?"

An expression that Kieran hadn't seen on Jordan's face before — panic, guilt — was immediately replaced by a non-committal shrug and frown.

"I don't know," Jordan said simply.

"My brother…" Kieran attempted to talk, to ask more questions, but he couldn't find the words. He felt as if Jordan was lying to him, thought he could see it in his eyes, but he didn't push it.

"I'm sorry, Kieran." Jordan sounded so broken. Desolate. Kieran could have pushed for more, part of him wanted to. Instead he reached out, instinct guiding his touch and pulled Jordan in for a close hug, allowing Jordan somewhere to hide his face even as his shoulders shook with sobs.

They had stood there for a long time, the graveyard truly empty, only the mound of dirt a reminder that a burial had even taken place. Even the staff had stood at a respectful distance, huddled in a small group — their backs to the two men.

When they had finally left the grave and mingled at the wake, they'd said no more on the subject. It was too raw. Kieran had tried to help where he could, but he'd only had a few weeks there before his first real job, a new post at the architectural firm Drewitt-Nate, required his return to London. Struggling with his own grief, he had felt his control slipping, his fury at what an idiot his brother had been burning keenly.

New to grief, his brother's memory washing Brad clear of negative traits, Kieran found it easier to look beyond Brad, to find someone else to blame. Jordan was supposed to have loved Brad. Damn. They'd been together since they were seventeen, when Kieran was only just a teenager. At the end of the day, *why* hadn't Jordan looked after him?

Three days after the funeral, the questions had become too much, and he'd set out to find Jordan. He had things to discuss.

He finally found his brother's partner in the yard, sitting under the tree in the corner, hidden from the view of the house, and he sat down opposite. So many memories arose when he thought of this tree, the large oak, gigantic before the first houses had been built, easily two hundred years old and steady as a rock. It held what remained of the tree house. It was the place where Kieran would sit and spy on his brother kissing his boyfriend, or girlfriend, of the week. The clubhouse was where he and Evan would sit and talk for hours about everything and nothing. He had finally realised he was gay on the scuffed timbers, and it was where he began to know that he loved his brother's now long-term boyfriend.

Jordan half smiled. "It's quiet here," he said simply.

"It's quiet in the house," Kieran pointed out.

"Different sort of peace here."

Kieran knew exactly what Jordan meant. The house was a sad house, full of unmentionable loss that just couldn't be handled. Out here, under the beautiful blue sky, was a place for memories. They sat in companionable silence for a good half hour, then Kieran began to talk, sharing memories of his brother. At first Jordan simply listened, but after a while, he began to add in his own memories, and they even laughed, although Kieran didn't see the laugh reaching Jordan's eyes. Kieran cried. It was the first time he'd let himself cry since he'd received the news that the brother he idolised had been taken far too young. Jordan did his best, pulling Kieran in for a hug similar to the one at the grave. He knew he couldn't provide any comfort because his own pain bit so deep, but he wanted to try to help.

Kieran sat back, trying to pull himself together, but something made Jordan grip tight, not letting him go…

Even now, Kieran couldn't recall why he had leaned in. He only knew that Jordan leaned in as well. They'd met in the absolute middle for the softest of kisses. It didn't matter who accused whom of taking the first step—it had been both of them, equally.

Both to blame…

As his thoughts turned back to the here and now, he pulled out his iPhone and typed out a quick resignation to Drewitt-Nate, citing family responsibility, and hovered only briefly over the send button. When the email had gone, he pushed the cell back into his jacket pocket. It hadn't hurt him as much as he'd thought it would to resign. He felt no worry that he might be giving up the start of his career. Kieran knew where he needed to be for his family. For Brad.

Kieran placed a hand on the cold stone of his brother's marker, tracing the letters of a name as familiar as his own.

'Bradley James Addison

Son, Brother, Friend'

His throat tight with pain and emotion, he closed his eyes against to the bright sun.

"I'm sorry I stayed away, Brad," he said softly, "so sorry."

Chapter Six

Two years earlier

Jordan shifted uncomfortably in the tight jeans and wife-beater Brad had picked out for him. He had added his opinion that Jordan was unable to look sexy without Brad's help. Jordan hadn't argued. His mind was on much worse things, like the place where he sat. He was like a fish out of water here in Lance's Bar, and he couldn't drink. He was not only driving, but he had to keep his wits about him.

Jordan was very aware of the reason Brad was here, and there was no way Jordan was going to go for a threesome, no matter what Brad said. It had been Brad's idea to drive three towns to the west to check out the place. Allegedly, all kinds of shit went down here, and Jordan hated the very idea of it. Something had been eating away at Brad recently. He was erratic and prone to temper, cementing the fact that there was no way Jordan was going to let the idiot go on his own. He was happy with Brad, in a committed relationship with a man he had loved since his early teens. Jordan didn't need some strange kid on his knees begging to suck him to define himself as a gay man.

Two hours earlier, he'd parked himself at the end corner of the bar, waiting for Brad to finish playing with that potential third. Jordan's heart ached, knowing that Brad felt their relationship needed an injection of excitement, burned that Brad obviously felt Jordan wasn't enough.

"I'm not gonna do anything," Brad had snapped when Jordan had asked where he was going, not liking the gleam in the flamer's eye. "Just gonna have fuuuuuunnn, Jordan."

Brad and what's-his-name had wandered off without a backward leer.

So Jordan had sat where Brad had left him, nursing a bottle, scribbling lists on napkins, trying damn hard to ignore what was happening and instead fixing his mind on work. He concentrated on the newest Addison contract, his first as sole foreman. Taking control of the whole project was a big responsibility, and Jordan wanted it done right.

Time had passed quickly, and Jordan had become totally focused on his lists and numbers. Then, out of the world beyond his thoughts, a single word caught his ear.

"Jordinaaaaa…"

Brad had returned, his voice mournful and low as he draped himself over Jordan and licked a stripe from jaw line to his cheekbone, nipping at the skin there.

"Wanna suck me?" he asked loudly, his hands diving to the front of his jeans and pulling at the buttons. "C'mon, need your fucking beautiful mouth on me." Brad bit down on Jordan's lip, drawing blood even as Jordan was trying to push him away. He winced at the bite, seeing dilated pupils and hearing the slur in Brad's words.

"What did he give you, Brad?"

"Good stuff, Jordina. Come on, get on your knees for me, baby. Your gorgeous lips… People wanna watch. They wanna see you suck me."

"Brad, you're high and drunk, man." Jordan glanced around Brad at the small group of men gathered behind them, all watching avidly as Brad got louder.

"Jordina…" By this time, Brad had his cock in his hands. His eyes were glazed over with drink-fuelled lust. Jordan loved Brad, but his behaviour tonight was over the line, even for Brad. Cursing, Jordan pushed Brad's cock back into his tight pants, ignoring Brad's pained squawk of protest.

Jordan heard someone very close to him say "prude" as he turned to leave, but he refused to rise to the bait. Grabbing the napkins he had been scribbling on, he stuffed them in his pocket. He dragged at spare material in Brad's shirt, guiding him out of the bar and into the cold night air, which Jordan desperately hoped would snap Brad out of being so drunk. Ignoring Brad's mumbled protests, Jordan hauled him by the shirt straight to their car.

"What did he give you? What was it? Brad?" Jordan propped him up against the side of the car, fishing in his pockets for the keys, wincing as Brad grabbed at his arms and pulled him in to grind against him.

"So pretty, Jordina," Brad slurred, a feral grin on his face. "Know you wanna get in my pants."

"Not now, Brad." Jordan managed to get the door open, balancing Brad against the hood. Brad was pouting, a spoilt kid's expression of frustration.

"Yes, now!" he demanded. He moved away from the door, swaying in the cold night, grabbing at Jordan's crotch. "If you loved me..."

Jordan sighed. *Not this again.* There wasn't any point in arguing with Brad. His partner's recent use of narcotics and growing dependence on alcohol always ended with Jordan being accused of cheating, or not loving Brad enough. The old argument. It always emerged from his subconscious when Brad was angry at the world. Thing was, it wasn't showing signs of stopping tonight—it was getting worse. He counted down in his head to the next inevitable topic. That Jordan wanted to leave, that Jordan wanted to finish the whole 'thing'.

"I bet you'd be on your knees if it was baby brother," Brad slurred.

Hang on... That was a new one.

"Kieran?"

"I saw ya...when you kissed him. Lucky fuck...my pretty brother."

"For God's sake, Brad, what the hell are you talking about?"

"You kissed him, 'member?" Brad poked at Jordan's chest.

"It was truth or dare, Brad, and it was years ago for fuck's sake! Shit, you *made* me kiss him." That was old news, a challenge on a dare to show Kieran how to kiss. Kieran had turned sixteen only the day before and had somehow got involved in Brad's version of celebrating the end of term. There had been too much alcohol, and on Jordan's part, a need to see if Kieran tasted as good as he looked. It was the kind of memory that went hand-in-hand with youthful indiscretions and teenage guilt.

"You didn't... Weren't meant to 'joy it."

"What? I didn't fucking enjoy it," Jordan lied, because that was what Brad wanted to hear. He didn't want to hear that Kieran had kissed with the enthusiasm of a virgin, but was so strong that the kiss had sent shockwaves up and down Jordan's spine. Brad didn't need to hear that, especially since he was leaning up against the car, off his head with some kind of narcotic and probably close to alcohol poisoning.

"I saw your hands," Brad said wildly. "All over him... holding his ass...grinding yourself..."

"Brad, that didn't happen," Jordan said patiently.

"Fuck him," Brad continued. "He has everything I wan', seeing the world... Fuck him. No ties to this fucking town, to a boring as shit life with a man that won't even suck me." Brad was deteriorating further into self-pity with each word, and Jordan knew his lover well enough that he had a small window of opportunity to wrestle him into the car and get them home to their small house on Main Street.

After manhandling Brad into the shotgun seat, he made sure the belt was clicked and tight across Brad before he climbed into the driver's side. In seconds, they were on the road, the lights of the club behind them, and finally, Jordan felt he could breathe. Was it so wrong to want to stay away from that particular club? That weird ass gay scene? Was it wrong to want more out of life? Stability, love, maybe a family of his own and not the exhibitionist sex that Brad demanded whenever he got drunk?

"Why wouldn't you?" Brad sniffed and wiped the back of

his hand across his face.

"Why wouldn't I what?"

"Want him. Love him. He doesn't know shit about my problems."

"Brad, for God's sake, stop acting like a child. I do not, nor have I ever loved or wanted, your little brother."

"Fuckin' Kieran," Brad muttered, "got off on you, I bet... in the shower, fucking hand job over the thought of your mouth on his cock."

Jordan tensed. This was another new one. Normally Brad would have subsided into sulking silence by now. "Shut the fuck up, Brad." Jordan really was starting to lose it now, his fingers gripping the steering wheel tight.

"Emails me, y'know, all the time. Tells me stuff, some shit about Evan and a gig, all this fuckin' crap about how happy he is seein' the world..." Brad scrambled to undo his seat belt, clumsy movements with alcohol and drug-fuelled anger radiating from him with a white hot heat. "He never said it, y'know, but he left because of you. Left me to do it all just 'cause he wants you. Bastard...left me."

"Brad, put your fucking belt back on or I will pull over," Jordan snapped quickly, trying to remember where the next turnout was in the unlit back road home to the Bay.

"He has everythin', y'know, everythin' I want —"

"Brad! Belt! And no, he doesn't have everything. You have a good life, Brad." Jordan didn't even know why he was defending their life together. Brad had been restless for a while, and Jordan sensed something had been eating away at Brad, but his boyfriend would never talk. He was forever clammed up tight.

"Always said he was going to leave, even in high school. Leave with that Evan ass and go see the world. He's got freedom. He's not tied down to...all these things I have to do, like I am."

"Brad, belt!" *Shit, Brad's on a roll.*

"I never wanted it. None of it. Never wanted a house. Never wanted to work on houses. Wanna see stuff like

Kieran. He's free. Just wanted to fuck you, thass'all. So pretty...love you." Brad was so wasted it was beyond a joke, and fear spiked in Jordan. Maybe he should be driving directly to the hospital instead of home.

"I'm pulling over."

"Little brother wants my boyfriend." Brad grinned in the half-dark as Jordan glanced over. "Can't have him," he slurred, and in a sudden lurch to the left, he bumped Jordan, the car veering to one side as Brad was suddenly all hands.

"Brad, please calm down." Jordan called upon his most calming voice, extricating his right hand from Brad's grip. Brad hadn't redone the belt and was now trying to dry hump him in a moving car. He needed to pull over, or the idiot was going to end up causing an accident. He slowed the car, moving to the shoulder of the unlit side road, the night black as ink around them...

* * * *

He hadn't seen the crater-sized hole in the blacktop that they said was the cause of it all. He'd only registered it as the car swerved under his grasp, hitting the shoulder and starting to slide. They hadn't been going fast, maybe only twenty, not speeding, and nothing was fast.

It had all been in a morbidly fascinating slow motion. Brad's hands had pulled at him, and Jordan had shouted something—he didn't know what—a warning maybe, even as the tree loomed there in front of them. It had been a Douglas fir. They had added that to the report.

They'd told him afterward Brad had never felt a thing. That his neck had snapped even as he was thrown through the front windshield, that he was dead before he came to a rest half in and half out of the shattered glass, his face a grotesque mask of red.

Toxicology had shown he was drugged and drunk, but that didn't matter, not to Jordan. The man he had loved, with whom he had planned a life, had died when Jordan had been driving.

If only he hadn't felt anything when he'd kissed Kieran, then he wouldn't have the weight of it bearing down on him so much. It was his fault. He should have been a better boyfriend, given Brad what he wanted, helped him.

Chapter Seven

Present day

When Jordan arrived back at the house, he debated whether or not to go in. He wondered if he was fit company, with the temper and the guilt and the God damned fear. He kept seeing Kieran removing the belt. God, what a freaking idiot. Kieran's reckless action sent Jordan into a tailspin. There had been a spark of survivor guilt caused by a flashback to the night of the accident. Jordan knew that. Knowing what the cause of his reaction had been didn't stop his hands from shaking as he gripped the wheel and crouched in the driver's seat.

He kept the engine idling, the impetus to run still in him. And, although he might never admit it, the rumbling engine soothed his mind even if it was held together more by prayer and bubblegum than anything. It was strangely comforting.

"Jordan?"

He started at the word, and shot a glance to his left. Phil stood next to the truck. Jordan immediately turned off the engine and climbed out of the vehicle. He could see Phil's enquiring glance as the man he thought of as his father squinted to see if Kieran sat in the passenger seat.

"Kieran went for a walk," he supplied helpfully. Jordan knew that Phil no doubt was wondering why Jordan had returned alone from the bank.

"Good." Phil paused, frowning like he was thinking up what to say. "Did it go…okay…at the bank?" He wouldn't look Jordan in the eyes, and Jordan wasn't feeling like it was his place to share the information. Everything related to the Addisons was Kieran's to deal with now.

Phil still looked at him, expecting information. When Jordan began to speak, he made sure that he let none of his surprise about the mortgage and his disappointment in being left out of the Addison's financial situation enter his voice. "It was fine. Kieran will talk to you later."

"Jordan." Phil's voice was strangely firm. "I'm glad you're here alone. It was actually you that I wanted to talk to."

"Shoot," Jordan said, leaning against the truck. Here it was. This was the moment when the axe fell. He'd been expecting it from the minute Kieran had walked through the door. Kieran was home, and it was going to be straight back to the old days when Jordan was the plus one in the Addison family. He wasn't going to fight for his position. He thought too much of the family that had virtually adopted him all those years ago. His never-absent guilt over what had happened to Brad reinforced his determination to leave without causing any upset to the people he held so dear.

"It's about the house and the company," Phil started. Jordan decided to nip in the bud whatever it was that Phil planned to say. He raised a hand to stop him.

"It's okay. I can be out of the garage room in a few days. But I'm going to need till the weekend to—"

"What?" Phil looked confused.

Jordan really hadn't expected that reaction. "I'm not going to cause any trouble. Things need to change now that Kieran's here."

"Now that he is, and to be honest we don't know if he is staying, things *will* change. You have carried this company for the last two years at least, since Brad... Since my health..." Phil's voice faded, and he gestured with a hand to indicate everything else. Jordan winced. Brad's death had affected Phil's health, his fragile heart nearly broken when he'd lost his eldest son.

"I wouldn't have wanted it any other way. When I think of the times you took me in when I was younger, I owe you so much," Jordan replied, still giving Phil an out if he needed it.

"You owe us? No..." Phil seemed suddenly flustered. "I just need to formalise it all." Phil's words emerged in a confused mumble. Subconsciously, he rubbed his hand on his chest. Jordan watched him do it. Knowing the cause of the new scars that ridged under the man's touch and hearing Phil's uncertainly brought Jordan out of his thoughts and into motion.

Insistently he guided the older man to the house. Jordan needed to sit Phil down. The last thing Phil needed was more stress. They had almost reached the front door when Phil stopped and half turned, clutching at Jordan's shirt.

"I can't lose another son, Jordan! Can you understand that?"

Jordan nodded, grief and guilt splitting him in half.

"I need to do everything I can to make Kieran stay."

"I understand." Jordan said these words because he thought they were expected of him somehow. He had always excelled at being the person who said the right thing, did the right thing.

"No, you don't understand. You can't. How can you?" Phil's voice was slurred with tiredness, and Jordan stopped any more talking by opening the door and ushering Phil indoors. They could talk later.

Anna was standing at the stove and immediately dropped everything to begin fussing around Phil, making him comfortable. Jordan hovered, in case he was needed, until finally the older man sat wrapped in a blanket.

"Jordan," he said simply as Jordan made his excuses to leave, hesitating, it seemed, until Jordan was looking directly at him. "Thank you, son."

Jordan nodded and half smiled, stepping to the side to let Hayley in as he left and the door shut behind him. Even as he made his way to his small apartment over the garage, Jordan's mind spun. He needed to decide what to do next. He had nothing to his name, but if Kieran was back, then there was no place for him with the Addisons, not even a place to live, really. He had always known that one day everything would catch up with him. He just hadn't expected it to be today, or for it to hurt so much.

* * * *

Kieran arrived home late, hobbling a little after the walk, his back stiff from leaning back against Brad's headstone, his throat raw from talking. Everything. He had told Brad everything. Every thought, every wish, every lie. The only other person that knew half of it was Evan. But not even Evan knew about the kiss under the tree house so soon after Brad had died.

"Hey."

Kieran stopped at the sound of Jordan's voice behind him in the half dark, and he turned to face his nemesis. The older man was sitting on the lower steps to the garage conversion, the air around him smelling faintly of cigarette smoke.

"Hey," Kieran responded carefully, digging his fingers into his pockets and trying to relax his stance.

"You okay?"

Kieran blinked at Jordan's careful question. *Okay*? He was far from okay.

"I just wanted to say something, quite apart from all the shit."

"Like?"

"Your family means everything to me. It is *because* they mean so much to me that I'm going to make it easy on everyone and go. I think you can help them if you just pull your head out of your ass long enough. All the resentment and shit between us will just get in the way, so I'm just going to walk."

Tension caused the breath to leave Kieran's lungs in one exhale. "Jordan, that is stupid. Look, wait—"

"I'm deadly serious about this, Kieran. It is *not* open for

65

discussion."

Jordan seemed set on what he was saying, and Kieran felt the jet lag wrap around him again as he attempted to find words. Leave? Why would Jordan believe he should leave? Kieran had been the one who'd fucked up.

He wasn't sure how long they stood there, but he was snapped out of his thoughts as Jordan said goodnight and turned to climb the iron stairs next to the garage. The converted apartment had become Jordan's home? When? What had happened to Jordan and Brad's house?

Confused and all but staggering under the weight of exhaustion, he pulled himself together enough to say, "Night," so softly that Jordan probably hadn't heard. He waited until the door shut. Squaring his shoulders, he turned back towards the main house. He would talk to Jordan in the morning, when he felt less raw, make him see he didn't need to be going anywhere.

The problem would still be there in the morning, and the jet lag was killing him, muddling his thoughts and making him unable to concentrate. He needed to sleep. When he walked into the kitchen, his mom was sitting at the table, nursing a coffee, her hands wrapped around the mug. She looked at him fondly, a smile on her face. Again he was caught by how tired she looked.

"Everything okay?" she asked carefully, in that non-intrusive way that his momma had about her.

"Everything's fine, Momma," Kieran lied, pushing his confused jumble of thoughts way down where he could try to forget about them. He strode across the kitchen and dropped a small kiss on her head. "I promise. I just went to see Brad. It's been a while. "

His mom smiled and shut her eyes for a few seconds. He'd almost reached the kitchen door when she spoke again, stopping him in his tracks.

"Can we talk?" his mom asked gently, indicating the seat opposite and rising to pour two fresh mugs of coffee. Kieran felt the pit of his stomach drop. He had avoided serious conversation with his mom for so long. So far, he'd managed to derail every reference to 'the talk' with the only person that could really see through him.

"Okay," he sighed, resigned, realising it was probably for the best that they get everything out in the open. He imagined she would want to know why he'd chosen a school overseas, why he hadn't come home, why she'd lost her middle child so very completely. He slid into the chair opposite her. He mimicked her earlier stance, wrapping his own hands around the hot mug as she had hers. He battled to keep his eyes open and to listen. She looked at him with that careful assessing gaze he had desperately tried to avoid for so long.

"It must be hard," she said simply, and Kieran wasn't quite sure what he was expected to say to that one.

"Hard? Nah, Mom, coming home is easy," he lied. Again.

"I don't mean coming home. Although I know that was hard as well. It must be hard to be this close to him." She couldn't have said a simpler sentence, but Kieran's reaction could not been more complicated. He blinked steadily, unable to think under the weight of his disjointed thoughts. He felt as if her words were a knife, and he had a bull's-eye painted on his chest.

"I don't understand," he finally said, speaking carefully. Maybe she hadn't meant what he thought she had.

"It must be singularly the worst thing to be so close to Jordan and not be able to tell him how you feel."

Kieran rocked back in his seat. *What the hell?*

"How do you—?" He wanted to say something. He wanted to ask her how she knew. Yet, if he did, if he gave his mom's question any weight at all, then surely he was admitting to another person, other than drunken ramblings with Evan, that he had feelings for Jordan.

"You thought we didn't know?" His mom didn't sound hurt, merely surprised at what he had just said.

"Momma..." Kieran really tried to string a sentence together, aware that now was the time that he shared his feelings with someone else. Suddenly he was desperate for her to see that he hadn't betrayed anyone, that he truly had left because he didn't want to hurt anyone. "It's not what you think."

"I think that you saw Jordan as more than your brother's boyfriend, Kieran. I think he holds a part of your heart that you will never get back from him." She said it with absolute conviction, and Kieran knew this was the moment. He couldn't keep it silent any longer if he tried.

"I loved him," he admitted. "I always did."

"And now?"

Kieran lifted his gaze. If he admitted it all to his mom, would she think less of him? Would she push him to one side, judge him for being the awful waste-of-space man that he knew he was?

"Momma..." he began. He had told Brad everything when he'd sat at his brother's grave. Most importantly, his mom deserved the truth. "I still love Jordan." It was such a simple statement, but instead of the weight lifting from him, a singular grief clutched at his heart. "What do I do?"

"Oh, baby." She grasped his hand tight, her hold reassuring and warm. "I don't have any easy answers for you."

Sudden horror snapped into Kieran, and the sadness in him died in a second under the weight of it. "Did he know?" *Did Brad know?* His mom looked at him with so much gentle love in her eyes that she didn't have to say anything. Brad had known.

"Brad sometimes said to me in private, especially the last few months before the accident, that he was no good for Jordan. Said he was pulling Jordan down."

"How?" Kieran hadn't been there to see it, didn't know the background.

Anna sighed. "I may have been his mother, but even I could see he was deliberately sabotaging what he had with Jordan. On a few occasions, he stated Jordan would have been better off with a different person, someone who really wanted him. Someone maybe like you."

Kieran closed his eyes briefly, the tears that choked his throat threatening to spill. "I never said anything to anyone, Momma. Not once."

"I know, baby."

"Why did Brad say that, then?"

His mom hesitated, and Kieran looked directly into her unwavering gaze. "It wasn't only you, Kieran. I think Brad wanted Jordan to be happy, and he couldn't make him happy anymore."

"What happened to him? To them? Why…when did it all go wrong?"

"Never doubt your brother, baby. He tried his hardest for us all. He…he invested money in a complex of apartments in Cooper's Heights. The company lost a lot of money."

"Hence the mortgage," Kieran said softly. His mom nodded.

"Your dad took the mortgage out to keep us in balance and never blamed Brad, but after that… I don't know how to explain, but everything starting spiralling downward. Brad would go out, mostly on his own, and drink. Jordan took up more and more of the responsibilities of the company, then when your dad became unwell…" Her voice tailed off, and Kieran filled in the blanks. His brother depressed, drinking, his dad too ill to carry the business, Jordan carrying the burden of everything.

A discordant thought niggled at the back of his mind, a tiny inconsistency in the whole story. He frowned, attempting to place his thoughts in order. Suddenly it came to him. The shock on Jordan's face in the bank—the disbelief that the company owed money. "Shit."

Anna frowned, and he squirmed. His mom still had the capacity to make him fidget when he cussed. "Sorry. I meant to say he didn't know, did he? Jordan, I mean. Brad and Dad…you… None of you told him about the money that Dad borrowed."

"No." A simple statement it might have been, but regret

coloured the words. "Jordan is such a fine man, and he was good for Brad. They had been happy, but things were hard for them. We were worried that it would be the last straw in their relationship. But at the end of it..."

"Mom?"

Anna squeezed his hand tight and gazed directly into his eyes. "That doesn't mean that I don't think you and Jordan wouldn't have made a good match as well. Brad was my wild child, and sometimes I would think he was too impulsive and too loud to be with Jordan. Jordan was the quieter man. Then I would see them hug, and despite the arguments and the tension, the love was still there."

"How can I...?" *Help me, Momma. How can I stop feeling this way?*

"There has always been something there between you and Jordan, something maybe more than brother and best friend. Brad may well have suspected."

"I stayed away."

"I know, sweetheart, and we missed you so much."

Chapter Eight

Jordan pulled out the bags, one battered case and a duffle—the same bags he had used through four years of college—and dropped them on the bed. He had sat for so long waiting for Kieran to come home, instinct telling him he needed to let Kieran know that family should come first. It didn't matter what part Jordan played in the life of this family. He had always kept himself apart, looking in from the outside. He crossed to the window, gazing over at the main house, a tumble of extended rooms, the light warm and inviting from the kitchen. Not since he had lost his own mom had he felt the grief as keen inside him. It was worse than when Brad had died. It was so much worse, but it wasn't grief edged with guilt. It was heartache and loneliness.

Kieran wasn't a boy anymore. He was a man now, a man who was more than capable of taking care of his family. It was time for Jordan to leave, and decision made, he circled on the spot, thinking about what he was going to take with him. He didn't have a lot. Everything he needed or wanted was in the main house. This place was nothing more than a place to sleep. He pulled clothes from drawers—work clothes and a few clean button-downs for business meetings. He lived in jeans and had a collection that ranged from work denim to pressed dark denim that passed for his version of a suit. That simply left his personal possessions. The newest Stephen King was lying on the bedside table, half read, but that was Hayley's actually, so he really needed to leave that.

He sighed as he picked up the one thing he really owned,

the simple silver frame, dull in the half light. In it was a picture of Brad and him at the last Fourth of July barbecue they had attended before the accident. Jordan squinted and looked closer, imagining he could see the unrest in Brad's eyes, the frustration in his boyfriend's mind. There was nothing there, just a smiling happy man who revealed nothing of his need to run, of his need for excitement, or for a life outside what he had with Jordan. Carefully he eased the picture out of the frame and dropped the picture to the bed. He would find a corner of his bags to hide the photo away where it would be safe. Sighing, he checked his watch. It was close to midnight now, and he wanted to be sure that he was there for the first bus in the morning. He had plans. It was maybe time for him to visit college buddies, do some travelling, anything—

The knock on the door broke through his thoughts. Hell, he must have been well out of it to not hear footsteps on the iron stairs. He crossed to open it, imagining it would be Hayley. She often came over to say goodnight after she'd been out. But he saw Kieran leaning against the top banister, he didn't know what to say.

"I didn't know you lived here now," Kieran started without hesitation.

"Only for the last couple of months," Jordan found himself answering, memories tumbling unbidden in his head of the house that he'd shared with Brad.

"I thought it was just a dumping ground. It always used to be." Was Kieran making small talk?

"Well, things change. What do you want, Kieran?" Jordan was aware his voice resonated with exhaustion. Sleep was a luxury that his injured hand would not let him have. He waited as Kieran went through several stages—a nervous shuffle from one foot to the other, a single hand swiping back through his blond hair, then a spine straightening with purpose.

"Can I come in?" Kieran finally asked. Jordan glanced behind him, to the small bedroom and to the bags that sat

72

on the covers.

"Er, it's not a good time," Jordan stuttered, moving to close the door and meeting Kieran's foot as it blocked the closing. "What the fuck, Kieran?" He opened it wide and angrily waited for a reason for Kieran being here. Kieran didn't hesitate, shoving Jordan out of the way and taking a step inside.

"I assume you're going?" Kieran wasn't wasting any time cutting to the chase, crossing to the bedroom and gesturing to the bags.

"Kieran…" Helplessly, Jordan watched as Kieran turned on him. Damn, he had really been hoping to leave without all this fucking drama.

"Don't."

"Don't go?" Jordan clarified, his eyes narrowing. "Kieran, I'm not doing this. I'm going, and I'm not arguing."

"No one wants you to go."

"At the end of the day, it's my choice."

"Is it my fault?" Kieran looked so innocent, his grey eyes filled with question.

"It's time for me to go." Subconsciously he slipped back to days when explaining things to the ever curious Kieran meant convoluted discussions on the roof of the garage looking up at a sky of stars. Kieran had always been one to ask questions, and to demand answers.

"Why?"

"I said I'm not doing this." It wasn't fair for Kieran to dig. Wasn't Jordan doing the right thing? Backing away, letting the family heal? What gave Kieran freaking Addison the right to question him? "It's for the best," he finally offered as a catch-all excuse.

"Bull. Shit," Kieran spat out. "You kept my family safe every day since Brad died, and I know that. I may not have been here, but don't ever think I didn't know that. They want you here. Hell, it isn't even a question they ask themselves. You are a son to them, a brother to Hayley." Kieran was evidently working up a rare head of steam, and

73

he was invading Jordan's personal space, jabbing a long finger at his chest. "If you leave now —"

"What, Kieran? What other emotional shit are you and your family going to dump on me to make me stay?" Jordan snapped, immediately regretting it as Kieran took a step back, a horrified look on his face.

"Is that what we do?" Kieran asked with shock in his voice. "Is that why you stayed here after Brad? After I left?"

"No," Jordan said tiredly, shaking his head. What was it that this man did to him that reduced him to a mess of neuroses? "I stayed because I wanted to. I love your family. They have been my family since Mom —" *Since my own mom died.*

Kieran seemed to think long on that one as both men stared at each other. Jordan didn't know what to say next. He had said his bit and wasn't sure there was anything else Kieran would want to hear. As he waited, he realised he could smell Kieran's scent, a combination of the night air and a woodsy scent that lingered from aftershave he had used before visiting the bank. Silently, he berated himself for being so stupid. He had no right to notice that Kieran smelt good, or that years away had meant the gangly teenager he once knew had really become a man. Tall, muscled, strong, different to how he remembered Kieran looking at the funeral, more focused maybe. He was still impossibly beautiful to look at — high cheekbones in a strong face and the grey of his eyes sparked with emotion. There was nothing of the kid that Jordan had known left in him, nothing of the smiling teasing brat who would not leave either Jordan or Brad alone any time he could find them.

It was Brad who had rocked Jordan's world with just a few simple words that seemed to mean nothing to him, words that meant more to Jordan than he could ever have realised.

"Kieran told me today that he thinks he is gay."

74

"Are you sure he isn't projecting? Brad, shit, he's only thirteen."

"Hell, I knew I was bi when I reached puberty."

"Brad, this is serious. This isn't a decision your little brother should be making based on hanging around with us, and for God's sake, maybe he is just with us too much. Maybe he should spend more time with girls."

"I think he's serious, Jordan. He'll need us, given that he doesn't have a ready-made gay boyfriend in his best friend to make it all easy."

"What do you mean by that? Was I just the easy option?"

"I didn't mean it that way, Jordan. You know I love you."

He snapped back into the room as Kieran continued the conversation. "Jordan, whatever you think of me, whatever happened between us in the past, however much you hate me, I will stay away from you. I won't push you, but just... Please don't go. Let's take some time and talk about things. I have so many questions, and I can't do this without you."

"Kieran..."

"It would break Mom's heart if you left," Kieran finished quietly, the final nail in the coffin, pulling the main front door behind him as he left Jordan standing in the room on his own.

Fuck.

Staying meant dealing with ghosts and memories he wished he'd never ever have to face. Going would be easy. He could travel around America, work temporary jobs, maybe find someone. Live. Love.

But he lived here, loved here. Was loved here.

Sighing, he realised there was no decision to make. He began to unpack. However hard he tried, though, he couldn't bring himself to reframe the photo. He simply slipped the six-by-four photo into his top drawer. He couldn't look Brad in the eyes, not even in a picture.

A shower would help, but he hadn't got around to installing one yet in the small apartment, not ever having been entirely sure if he was staying here permanently in the garage conversion or whether he was going to find somewhere he could afford to rent. Of course, not taking any kind of salary from the company meant that was unlikely to ever happen that he could afford rent anywhere. He usually made use of the main bathroom in the house, but he decided he couldn't take the risk tonight of running into Kieran. It had never been a problem before. He used the boys' old bathroom with the names *Brad* and *Kieran* still carved into the door. He couldn't conceive of sharing a bathroom with Kieran now. What if Kieran walked in on him naked?

He couldn't keep his mind from picturing Kieran naked in the shower. What if he went over to the house now and opened the bathroom door and Kieran was showering, the glass showing every single muscle and every inch of skin? What if Kieran was covered in soap, slick and slippery, his head tipped back under the cascading water, his eyes shut and his lips parted on a breath? What if Jordan just froze to the spot, unable to move? What if he simply stood there and watched, becoming impossibly hard, and pushing his hand down his pants? How easy would it be to circle his cock and press hot fingers to the damp tip of it to smooth the way?

What if Kieran saw him and climbed out of the shower with water droplets tracing paths around and across each sharp angle and tight muscle? What if Kieran dropped to his knees at Jordan's feet, his mouth greedy, closing around the head of Jordan's cock, using his oh so fucking clever tongue, pulling, sucking and licking Jordan to orgasm?

Jordan groaned as the images flew at him. He could almost feel hot lips around him, and grey eyes staring up at him, full of lust and want.

When Jordan came over his clenched fist, there was only one name on his lips. *Kieran*. But no one would hear it over the harsh groan that was pulled from his chest at the same time.

Brad. I'm sorry.

Chapter Nine

Kieran couldn't sleep. He wasn't entirely sure whether it was being home, or whether it was Jordan's unsettling admission that he had felt emotionally blackmailed into remaining with the Addisons. Both things seemed to weigh heavily on his mind and chased him from his bed at just after five in the morning to stand at his window and stare out at the low mist clinging to the May morning. Tension snagged between his shoulders, and with sudden inspiration, he pulled on sweats and an old tee and grabbed his sneakers. His back still ached from sitting at the grave, and having had no sleep didn't help the ache. He swallowed some painkillers, and began a series of stretches designed to relax the ache in his muscles. He felt the need to go out on a run, nothing too heavy, just around old familiar streets to try to gauge how things had changed in the time he'd been away.

He bypassed running anywhere near the cemetery, concentrating instead on the gradual climb to Cooper's Peak, his breath quick and free in the morning. What had Jordan meant last night? That backing away from the Addison family would be the best? The best for whom exactly?

It was different running here than in London. The old city had been busy even this early, a mishmash of humanity scurrying in and out of tube stations, intent on destinations he could only guess at, a surprise around every corner. London contrasted with the quiet peace of the Vermont day to the point where his hometown was almost too quiet. Thinking of Jordan and the feelings that churned inside Kieran as soon as he laid eyes on him, he realised all he felt was confused. Seeing Jordan again was hard. His face gaunt and tired, the older man's eyes had sparked with accusation as he asked why Kieran had come home. Sorrow and shame dragged feelings of regret from where they'd been hidden for so long. He wanted to be sorry, wanted to apologise for what he'd done — shit, he wanted to apologise for the things he hadn't done.

His iPod switched to a song that only Evan could have loaded on to it before he'd left their small flat — *Leaving on a Jet Plane*. *Idiot*, he thought affectionately, pangs of missing his best friend just adding another layer of misery onto his already burdened list of things he found bewildering.

He turned onto Main Street, dodging a cat that was rooting through a sack of rubbish outside the small fast food restaurant by the traffic lights. Not one of the shops in the randomly placed row of them showed any signs of life. No early morning coffee, or muffins, or the noise of people talking on cell phones. He checked out Alvin's place as he passed. Alvin's, a barber's shop, belonged to an old school friend's dad. He caught a glimpse of himself as he used to when he passed as a teenager. He was taller, wider, older, but his hair remained that same messy array of streaked blond.

He shook the images of his youth from his head and checked out each shop down the main street. Real maple syrup, skiing, stone fences, fall colour... He knew from experience that these were the things people identified with Vermont, but to him, looking at Cooper's Bay in isolation, it was family, familiarity — home.

Leaving Main Street, he took the turn to the bay that gave his town its name. Not a bay, really, but a shoreline on Lake Champlain. One person was throwing sticks for their dog into the stillness of the water, and Kieran nodded in passing. He didn't recognise them, but why would he? It had been so long since he had any kind of routine exposure to this small town. Half an hour into the run, when he saw the first car on the road into town, he doubled back to home, realising he had actually pushed back the worries with the rhythm of his feet on the road. It was a good feeling.

He could compartmentalise Jordan. He didn't need to act on any lingering attraction he may have for his brother's partner. His dead brother.

"Kieran, can you make sure you're in the house at ten?"

Jordan's voice forced its way into his thoughts as Kieran stopped at the yard gate to stretch out the muscles after his run. It startled him, and he blinked wide as his brain tried to catch up with his surprise. Jordan was dressed similar to him in sweats and an old tee, clearly just starting his own exercise. That had always been one thing they'd had in common—an enjoyment of the early morning run.

"Your dad wants a family meeting," Jordan added with a shrug.

"Yeah, I'll be there." Stupid response. Of course he'd be there, and why did Jordan's question have an edge to it? "Will you?"

"Your dad wants me there. And in any case I guess I need to hand some stuff over."

"What stuff?" Kieran asked because he thought he ought to. He didn't really want to have to stand here and listen to Jordan's soft voice anymore—his gorgeous, low, rumbly voice. Jeez, when had he started waxing lyrical over things like a guy's freaking voice? He was clearly losing it. The edge had gone in that low growl, but there was a resignation, a sadness in Jordan's tone that made Kieran wonder what the hell was going on with Jordan. Self-preservation and an uncomfortable erection hidden only by the baggy sweats meant he really had to make a move away from here.

"See you at ten," Jordan finally said, clearly choosing not to answer the whole 'stuff' question.

"Ten." Kieran nodded, shifting on the balls of his feet slightly, then he waited, unsure what to say next. Jordan nodded once then left the property in a slow jog.

Ten then.

He went into the house and snagged a bottle of ice water

from the fridge before moving to his room and stripping for the shower. The water would wash away the sweat, and he could maybe deal with the small, or not so small, problem of the fact that just the sound of Jordan's voice made him hard.

The water was hot and his orgasm was quick with the image of Jordan in his head, though he would deny it if asked. When he slumped on his bed wrapped in a towel, he knew he needed to talk to someone. His emotions were out of hand.

He had things to decide. His job wasn't open for him in London, but he could continue his career, get it back on track by contacting companies in Richmond.

He imagined the offices of Drewitt-Nate, and Tamsin at her desk, filing her nails, still passing on calls without identifying the caller. He imagined his desk in the corner — a cubicle, nothing more than three partitions closing off his drafting table and the designs that would be scattered upon it. Not his designs. Senior partner work on which he checked angles and structure, never more than that. He hadn't created anything new, nothing tangible, probably wouldn't until his informal apprenticeship was completed. Another six years. He had been alone, apart from Evan, adrift and so damn sad to be away from his family.

His momma knew, therefore his dad must know, and he assumed Hayley had noticed the same things their momma had — she was scarily similar to Mom in so many ways.

He wasn't going back to London. If the worst he had to do was fight attraction to someone who clearly had no interest in him and was entangled in memories of his brother then he could handle that. He would have to. What kind of man would he be to abandon his family now? He may have left after the funeral, but that had been wrong. He was staying here. It wasn't a decision he really needed to make. It was simple and clear cut. He was back home to stay.

There was only one cloud on the horizon in the form of the one person he'd abandoned back in England, his best friend since kindergarten. Evan needed to know his decision. Lying back on the soft pillows, he grabbed his cell from the nightstand and speed dialled number three — Evan Montague Owens, complete idiot and the best friend a man could ever have.

"Hey," he said firmly, not allowing any doubt to creep into his voice from the very beginning of this conversation. Evan sounded winded, and Kieran guessed he had either caught his friend at the gym or maybe Annabelle from flat two had finally given in to Evan's pestering for no complications sex.

"Hey, K... Hold up, bro..." The phone went dead for a few seconds, then his friend's voice was back. "Twelve miles on the running machine. Beat that, you pansy-assed ten-miler asshole." Same old Evan, fiercely competitive and so very capable of bringing a smile to Kieran's face with nothing more than a single snarky comment.

"Screw you. Five miles in the Vermont air, dickwad," Kieran offered in return. The familiarity of exchanging insults was a nice one.

"Fucker."

"Gorgeous lake, blue skies."

"College girls?" The campus for Champlain College was close by. "Running college girls?" Evan suggested, then added. "Naked ones preferably, and in pairs."

"Nah, but fuck, Evan, there was this guy, and his cock —"

"No, no, no, no, not listening to your depraved shit, gayboy." They laughed, and Kieran managed to hold off what he really wanted to say for at least another thirty seconds before it just became too much to hold in.

"I'm staying," Kieran blurted out. He could have sugar-coated it, maybe worded it a little differently to take the edge off it, but at the end of things, Evan deserved honesty.

"I already served notice on the apartment," his best friend said patiently.

"You did?"

"I booked a flight. I'm coming home to stay. Someone

needs to even out the gay in Cooper's Bay."

"Evan..." How the hell did he respond to that one?

"No rom-com shit, dude."

"Your career—"

"No such thing here," Evan responded, and Kieran winced inwardly. Neither he nor Evan had really made a huge splash in London. "Kee-ran, I mean it. I'm coming home to stay."

Kieran hesitated. He knew Evan was coming home. They had agreed a visit would be good, that Evan needed to touch base. But to stay? What had prompted that? Was it him? Was it his fault? "Ev?"

"Man, I'm tired of scraping and working shit jobs at the paper. I want to write, I want to see my dad, even if he is an asshole. I want to be in a place that is home, a proper home." Evan sounded tired, and Kieran wasn't sure exactly what to say. Selfishly he wanted his best friend here, wanted him back in Cooper's Bay.

"I want you to come home." Kieran desperately fought back the urge to add anything along the lines of 'It'll be good to have you here'.

"How's your dad?"

"Holding on, doing okay."

"Your mom?"

"Struggling a bit."

"How about that fine jailbait sister of yours?"

Kieran smirked to himself—even, to his relief, got close to actual smiling at that. Evan's attraction to Hayley was well documented back in time and littered with refusals and rebuffs. "She's dating and well out of your reach."

"Damn her," he chuckled. There was a pause, and he cleared his throat, clearly deliberating on the next words out of his mouth.

"Pick me up from the airport?"

"Text me the flight details. I'll be there."

Chapter Ten

Going to the family meeting was hard. Jordan didn't even know why he'd been asked to come, refusing to believe he was going to be told to leave in such a cold, impersonal way. He sat to one side, Kieran diagonally across to him, neither of them looking at the other. It was tense, and Jordan was feeling the stress. He didn't really want to be there, but Phil had come over to his room and practically begged him to attend. Apparently there were decisions to be made, and Jordan was part of those decisions. Kieran seemed equally uncomfortable, twisting a paperclip into nothing more than broken pieces as Phil gathered up papers and now sat like he was going to proclaim a sentence.

"I guess I should start with the fact that I spoke to Kieran yesterday before he went with Jordan to the bank. I told him what I was proposing, and he is fully behind everything I want for Addison Construction, and indeed for this family." He paused, and Jordan chanced a quick look at Kieran. He was staring at Phil with a look on his face that Jordan could not, for the life of him, get a handle on. "Hayley has indicated no interest in working on the physical side of the company, and it's her place to decide whatever she wants."

"Too right," Hayley said firmly.

"However, Kieran and I don't want to discount any legacy that AC may provide for her, and I have drawn up papers to split the company equally."

Jordan swallowed. It was a legacy the Addison children should all be sharing, Brad as well.

"I had my lawyer draw up papers to transfer control, and I need your signatures to make it happen." Phil paused, passing papers to Kieran who picked them up and flicked through them. "Kieran has confirmed he will be staying and working here. He has some strong ideas about merging our detailing work and his own skills in architecture." Kieran signed and passed them to Hayley who added her own signature. With no prompting, she slid the papers towards Jordan, who just stared at them.

"You need to sign," Hayley said gently, even as Jordan looked at her, then to Kieran then back at the papers. His name was at the bottom. *Jordan Robert Salter.*

"I don't understand," he said. Hope was coursing through him, but denial was his friend. This couldn't mean what he thought it might mean.

"When I said I wanted this to go to family—Jordan, you are family to me...to us," Phil said earnestly, and Anna leaned against her husband, a smile on her face. Jordan had no words. Looking back down at the papers, his eyes moved to his name under Kieran's sprawling signature, and he hesitated, the nib of the pen resting on the thick paper. What did this mean? Adding his signature here was possibly the biggest decision of his life. Much bigger than not leaving after Brad died. Staying meant dealing with his guilt and denying his attraction for Kieran. It meant making choices for the company that would affect his own ownership. He glanced at the percentages, a third of the company each. A third. His and Hayley's and Kieran's. Salary from profits for him and Kieran. *His.* Grief clogged his throat, and he didn't have the words. He hesitated—not actually putting pen to paper. Was this really what Kieran wanted? To be tied to a man he couldn't even talk to, let alone work alongside?

"This is a decision you all made?" Jordan asked gently, looking up at each person in turn. Phil and Anna were smiling, Hayley nodded, but Kieran would not look him in the eyes. Was Kieran even aware of what Phil had decided? Phil had said Kieran knew, that Kieran had agreed, but had he been pressured into it? "Kieran?"

"It was a unanimous decision," Kieran answered, finally looking directly at Jordan, a spark of something in his eyes. Jordan couldn't work it out. Was Kieran angry or sad? Had he made the decision under duress? There was nothing there, just a focused stare, and suddenly he knew he wasn't going to question this change in fortune. Phil and Anna had really been the only family he had ever known, and he looked on Hayley as a sister.

So he had to deal with Kieran. He could do that. He could push all his feelings for the younger man to one side and lock them in a box alongside the guilt tied to Brad. Within seconds, his looping signature was added to the papers. Then he stood abruptly and crossed to the coffee maker where he poured a full mug then leant back against the counter. Should he say something? A thank you? Maybe even somehow retract his signature? Was that even possible?

Kieran joined him at the counter, grabbing his own mug and bumping shoulders with Jordan before sipping at the fragrant brew. Jordan wasn't sure how to react to that one.

"We need to talk, get some idea of where we are going here," Kieran murmured softly.

How was that for a loaded statement? Kieran placed a firm hand on his dad's shoulder, a reassuring touch, then he gathered up all the papers in front of Phil and pushed them into the folder that had sat to one side.

"Let's get out of here," he said, obviously not expecting an argument, and left the kitchen, the door swinging shut behind him. Jordan wasn't going to argue, but he couldn't seem to make his feet move to follow his now business partner out of the house.

"I want to say thank you—"

Anna stopped him with a quiet "hush now" and pulled Hayley out of the kitchen, leaving Phil and Jordan in some kind of weird face-off. Phil still sat, and out of deference for his illness, Jordan slid back into the chair opposite him.

"You and Brad were as good as married," Phil started

carefully, his features relaxed into a small smile. "I never could understand how I managed to produce not one but two gay sons, but I never for one moment questioned it. Not even when Brad brought you home as his boyfriend rather than just his friend that first time..." He tilted his head. Reminiscing was something he was doing an awful lot of these days, and it scared Jordan to see this once strong man so lost in the past.

Jordan remembered the day clearly. Brad had been in his class from when Jordan had been six and, for some strange reason, had befriended the shy bookworm who spent most breaks in tears in the boys' room. They had never looked back, not really. They simply gravitated through the years with ease from buddies to lovers with no conscious thought.

"You had no momma, and Anna adored you, wanted to keep you, cried some nights when she sent you back to your dad."

"She did?" Jordan hadn't known this. He had no idea why Anna would even worry. His dad may well have been a closet alcoholic and a bit of a deadbeat, but he had never actually physically harmed his son in any way.

"Said it was way too much responsibility for a boy to be looking out for his dad so much."

Jordan shrugged—it hadn't been that hard. After all, he'd always had the Addison's house to visit with its cookies, its love and its laughter. Maybe that was why he and Brad had stayed so close. It was Jordan who had clung to Brad, but who would blame the poor kid from the other side of town? If their relationship had been built on nothing but awesome sex and Jordan's need for home then at least they had been happy. Jordan had given Brad everything he wanted. Literally everything...except the one thing Brad had clearly wanted at the end. Freedom from being tied to the business, freedom to see other countries, even maybe freedom from Jordan.

"I was okay," Jordan offered softly, "but it was always my home here."

"And that was right, you had a home here. You will always have a home here. You are in our hearts, Jordan, and now, with the papers, you are now officially by law as much a part of this company and our lives as Kieran and Hayley."

"Phil?"

"Son?"

"Why is there a mortgage on the house?" Jordan hadn't wanted to phrase it that way, but bluntly was the way it spilled from his lips. For his part, Phil just looked suddenly very defeated.

"I didn't mean to keep it from you, Jordan. It wasn't my intention, but I didn't want you—" Phil stopped, coughing into his fist then leaning back in his chair.

"Want me what?"

"I didn't want you feeling less for Brad."

"Brad did something?"

"Some big property investments went south, maybe a year or so before he—before we lost him. I borrowed enough so the company didn't lose out from those decisions."

Jordan nodded. He'd had some suspicions something was horribly wrong, but Brad had always shrugged him away. After all—as Brad had often reminded him at the end, just before he'd died—it wasn't *his* company, and the Addisons weren't *his* family. He remembered papers that Brad had left lying on the side of the kitchen counter, and his lover's downturn in mood after a heated phone conversation with who knows who on the end of the line. He had never known the extent, though, of what Brad had done, never knew it could be enough to pull the company down. He should have asked. He'd tried, but not hard enough.

"How much did he lose?"

"Just short of two hundred thousand," Phil replied sadly, and Jordan had to act really well to cover the shock at what his lover had done. The pressure on Brad had to have been incredible. Was that the reason he had become this creature of sensation? Was he hiding his fear and pain behind the wall of apparent indifference he had been building against Jordan? *Shit*. Jordan sighed inwardly. Now was not the time to be thinking on these things, and he pulled himself back to concentrate on the crux of what Phil had revealed.

"Okay. I wish I had known about it before going to the bank." He suddenly realised what he had said. "I didn't mean — it's really nothing we can't handle now that we all know." It was Phil's turn to nod, at first frowning, then his face creased into a hundred laugh lines as he smiled.

"You're good for this family, Jordan."

* * * *

Kieran leant back against the truck, checking his cell for messages. Evan had sent him the usual jokes, comments and one last text with an arrival date. He closed his eyes briefly. For all his sins, and the trouble Kieran invariably found himself in because of his friend, he missed Evan like he would miss a limb. Damned idiot had blown the last of his money on first class travel. *'If a boy has to come home, he needs to come home in style.'* Evan had a way of making things seem not so hard.

Jordan didn't follow him out of the house straight away, but Kieran wasn't concerned. He imagined Jordan had some things to say to Dad and so he waited. He tilted his head back and closed his eyes, his head bursting with ideas about what Jordan and he could do for the company — his designs, Jordan's skill at carpentry. Somehow they could pull this company together. From his dad's perspective, Jordan had done a damn fine job keeping the whole thing going during times of recession, and as the economy started to strengthen, it could only mean good things for them all. Kieran had yet to see the whole proof of that, but he didn't doubt his dad for one minute.

"Where are we going?" Kieran was startled as Jordan came to a halt next to him, opening his eyes and blinking at the light.

"Dad was telling me about the Johnson house that came on the market for renovation."

"It's too big for us," Jordan replied quickly, but Kieran just held up a hand to stop him.

"Dad said that, but I did some research—"

"Kieran, this isn't going to go well if you discount everything your dad or I say. We already looked. We know this restoration from the ground up, with all its problems. Shit, Kieran, the amount of money we would need to take this on is way out of our reach." Kieran winced at the immediate anger and defence in Jordan's urgent response.

"I'm not discounting anything from you or Dad, I'm not. Please just listen to me." There was a pause, Jordan seeming to weigh up what Kieran was saying then he shrugged to indicate Kieran should continue. "Can we drive up there, talk on site?"

Jordan said nothing in return, just climbed into truck, indicating Kieran should join him. He supposed that was one step in the right direction—at least they were in the truck. His hand had healed enough that he could drive and that at least was one tick in the plus column.

"Put your seat belt on," Jordan said firmly as soon as Kieran clambered up in the cab.

"Dude, I am *twenty*-six, not six," Kieran muttered, slumping back in the seat, reverting to the childhood hate of being ordered around by a big brother as quick as you could say *childish*.

"Put the belt on," Jordan insisted.

"It's only like two miles to the Johnson place." Kieran realised he was very close to sounding like he was whining, which undermined being a grown up and convincing Jordan that the Johnson place was a good project for AC. Jordan turned in his own seat and blinked steadily, and Kieran realised that the truck was going nowhere until he had his belt firmly in place.

"All right already," he muttered and pulled the belt across his chest, making sure it was fastened properly then deliberately staring out of his window.

Within ten minutes, they had arrived, parked outside the disused, dishevelled old lady that was the Johnson mansion. It was built in the Federal style, with its light, curved and delicate detailing inspired, Kieran knew, by buildings of ancient Rome. He was always stunned when he saw her. He stopped momentarily to admire the beautiful proportions with the central front door the focus, framed by three-quarter length sidelights and thin pilasters. The fan light above the door was delicate and intricate, and the Palladian window on the second floor above the door glinted in the light despite the fact the glass was broken in many places.

"Did you know Federal was the first major architectural style in Vermont?"

"I researched," Jordan replied, sarcasm in his voice as he came around from the other side of the truck. Kieran just ignored him. He had things he needed to say, stories he needed to tell.

"When I was in high school, I researched the architectural pattern books published by master builders in the late seventeen hundreds."

"Always the geek."

Kieran chose to again ignore the sarcasm as it was gently served to him with little malice.

"It was *this* actual house that was the centrepiece of the assignment."

"A-grade stuff there, Mr Architect."

"Do you want to talk about this or not?"

"I'm listening." Jordan encouraged him with a smile and a nod.

"What do you see when you look at her?" Kieran asked softly. He took a few steps closer, his boots crunching rubbish left by kids, evidence of dares to visit the mansion that was known locally as the *ghost house*. He looked down, seeing the detritus of disuse and wrinkled his nose in disdain. It was an insult to have the old lady sitting in such chaos and clutter.

"What do I see?" Jordan frowned. He took the few steps through the tangle of creepers to the stairs leading to the entrance door, crouched down and touched aged and cracked wood. Something scurried past his feet, but he didn't seem to notice, and for that, Kieran was pleased. "A money pit, ruin, destruction, abuse—" He paused, and Kieran joined him, crouching down and touching the same wood.

"What else?"

Jordan looked up at him briefly, and Kieran felt a surge of affection for what he could see in Jordan's eyes. Enthusiasm.

"History. I can feel the history in the grain, the peeling paint, the art that made these steps." He stood abruptly, grabbing hold of the railing and carefully taking the six brick-surrounded steps to the door. "I see where I could bring the girl back, have the creation under my hands, renovate and make it new." He flushed red with obvious discomfort as he turned to face Kieran, and it was all Kieran could do not to kiss him there and then on the edge of the history beneath his feet.

"That's what I see too, Jordan. Quite apart from the basics, the Federal style represents the seventeen nineties or thereabouts—after the Revolution, before the Civil War, when the future of the country was uncertain. When I look at this house, I see the grand old lady she used to be, and I want to sketch and change and work and make her whole again."

"We have to be practical here, Kieran. I'm one man—"

"Two. There's two of us, Jordan."

"No offence, but I'm guessing the last time you worked construction was when you were seventeen." Jordan took a step closer and grasped Kieran's hands, turning them so he could see the palms. Though he wanted to pull back, Kieran let him inspect. "These are hands that draw, not hands that build."

Irritated, Kieran pulled his hands away, cursing inwardly that he had given such an obvious sign of how affected he was at Jordan's hold on him. "I'm not some pencil pusher, I can *do* physical work you know," Kieran snapped back, more in defence and for something to say than anything else.

Jordan winced at the words that Kieran knew must hurt.

"So what is your idea here?" Jordan finally asked, thoughtfully tracing a glass panel with his fingers.

"I design, we submit, we undercut everyone, we don't take a salary, we pull AC out of the pit."

"No salary," Jordan said flatly.

Great. Jordan had to pick on that one. Kieran really thought he might be able to slip that one past him without him noticing until they had a few minutes to really discuss it. He thought maybe after he looked at the finances tonight he could get it so Jordan didn't have to lose money. Maybe it could just be him. Of course the conversation was coming sooner than he wanted.

"I thought—" Jeez, how did he phrase this without coming across holier than thou? "For the company, I could skip paying myself for maybe three months, push it forward and get some kind of cushion. Thought the company could maybe owe you, owe us."

Jordan stiffened at the words, crossing his arms over his chest, and Kieran prepared himself for an argument. There was none.

"Okay."

"Okay?"

"Look, Kieran, whatever you think, I *will* do anything to make this work." He held out his right hand, and Kieran clasped it with his, a firm handshake, an agreement.

"For Brad," Jordan added, and Kieran dropped his grip and took a step back.

"Yeah."

Chapter Eleven

Jordan was tired. Exhausted. His hand and wrist ached, his body felt like it had been run through with lead, but his mind was buzzing and he couldn't sleep. He sat on the iron steps by the garage, leaning back and looking up at the stars. There were so many confused images in his head that he couldn't begin to think about the renovations or anything for the future. He was on his second beer.

"Beer at midnight? I thought by now you would have given those up." Soft words, but Jordan started in surprise at Kieran standing there looking down at him, his hands pushed in his jeans pockets and his face half in the shadows.

"Several times," Jordan responded with a hint of humour in his voice. "Why are you out here?"

"Couldn't sleep. Too much in my head, so I drew some stuff, didn't work, saw you here—" Kieran shrugged, like that explained everything.

"Drafting, or sketching?" Jordan was curious. Kieran was a gifted artist and could capture scenes in beautiful intricate detail. He wondered if his lover's brother had kept it up. He shifted on the stairs, the iron starting to become uncomfortable to sit still on, even more so when Kieran decided to sit next to him, his thigh touching Jordan's and the smell of shampoo drifting down with him. He had obviously showered before coming out.

"Mmm, some sketching, and a bit on the house. I have some ideas. There is a lot of sixties shit in the house, orange walls, a plastic kitchen. We need to rip it all out." Kieran waved his hands expansively, knocking Jordan's sore wrist, causing him to wince at the pain. He wriggled back a bit, but Kieran caught his hand, looking at the bandage, probably imagining the injury under the grubby grey day-old material.

"Dude," Jordan murmured, pulling his hand free, and Kieran just smiled that stupid smile of his, the one that was apology and laugh all in one. The one Jordan remembered from the first kiss.

"Sorry," Kieran offered, and leant back, silently contemplating the stars Jordan had been examining.

Jordan had nothing else to say and shifted to draw up his knees, popping the tab on another beer. That damn kiss was never going to leave him. Brad and his half-assed dares.

"It's all he needs, Jordan. Just a kiss from a boy then he'd know."
"You do it then."
"Yeah, right, like incest is going to help him see if he is gay or not."
"I'm not kissing him, Brad."
"Have another beer."

That night, the night of Kieran's sixteenth birthday, too much alcohol on his part and too much innocence for Kieran had been a bad combination, and there it was. The dark, the stars, the beer and the singularly most perfect kiss Jordan had ever had. He shuffled back again, realising he was getting hard — over memories, for fuck's sake, just memories. Then guilt chased the arousal, and as quick as he was hard, it was gone again.

"The kiss..." he began softly, causing Kieran to lower his head from looking at the sky and turn his face away.

"The kiss?"

"On your sixteenth."

"Oh, *that* kiss." Kieran emphasised the fact it was the kiss at his birthday and not the one in the days following the funeral.

"I'm sorry," Jordan offered carefully.

"Don't be sorry, Jordan." Kieran sounded fierce.

94

Don't be sorry? Of course Jordan knew he should be sorry. It had been a nasty joke to play on the kid brother of his best friend.

"Whatever. I'm sorry."

"Well, I'm not." Kieran scrambled to stand, his long limbs uncurling until he stood to full height, blocking any light from reaching Jordan. In an abrupt motion, he leant down and twisted his fingers into Jordan's jacket, pulling him ever so subtly towards him and placed dry lips firmly against Jordan's. It was nothing more than the shock of touch, but when Jordan opened his mouth on a gasp of surprise, Kieran pressed his advantage to taste Jordan. It was quick, impulsive and hot, and Jordan chased for the kiss as Kieran pulled away, realised what he was doing and jerked back in abject horror.

"Kieran, fuck."

"The best kisses of my life, Jordan. All three of them." He turned and stalked away, but not before Jordan heard the pain in Kieran's voice.

Jordan lurched to his feet, blinking at the head rush and grabbing hold of the stair rail to balance himself.

"Kieran!" There was no way the bastard was going to get away with a kiss and run like that without one damn long conversation that started with the question "What the fuck?"

Kieran didn't stop walking, even though Jordan knew he must have heard him.

"Kieran!" Then, to himself, he muttered, "Oh no, you don't. You don't walk away."

"'Night, Jordan," Kieran called, voice clearly shaking as he disappeared around the side of the house towards the rear door. Jordan didn't pause one moment, and in a few quick strides, he rounded the same corner.

And almost slammed straight into Kieran, who had stopped just out of sight. He was leaning against the house, looking up into the night sky, and he hunched his shoulders as Jordan slid to a halt in front of him. It was the classic Kieran

Addison defensive stance. He looked impossibly young as he stood there, and something clenched in Jordan's chest. He was only a few years younger than him, but he didn't have the responsibility on him that Jordan had. How could he do this to Jordan? Try to turn rocks to expose the things that should never be acknowledged? He was flooded with emotion that hurt, a combination of anger and something else. Confusion.

"What the hell was *that*?" Jordan snapped, jabbing Kieran's broad chest with the tips of his fingers.

"If you need to ask then I wasn't doing it right," Kieran replied enigmatically, grabbing at the offending fingers and drawing Jordan's whole hand into one of his. Jordan quickly shook it free then pushed his hands deep into his loose jeans pockets, wincing at the pain in the injured one.

"Don't fuck with me, Kieran."

"I'm not. Believe me, I'm not," Kieran closed his eyes and banged his head back on the stone, once, twice, a third time.

"Was that some kind of head-game? 'Cause if it was, then congratulations, you totally won some points."

"No head-games, Jordan," Kieran sighed, cautiously reaching a hand out to touch Jordan mid-chest, gently establishing a connection. "You're never going to see it."

"See what?" Even though he asked, in his heart he already knew what Kieran was talking about.

"We need to clear the air before we start the work, before we put too much more of ourselves into this."

"Clear the air? And how did *that* back there clear the air?" How was Kieran not seeing how much trouble this could cause? Why dig up this stuff now?

"Do you know how hard this is for me?" Kieran was pleading, his eyes closing briefly. He clearly didn't want to talk here, but there was no way that Jordan was letting this lie.

"You wanted to 'clear the air', so you thought it was a good idea to kiss me? You freakin' kissed me and brought back every damn thing I don't want to remember? That's clearing the air? Damn it, Kieran!" Jordan pounded his fist against his thigh rather than against Kieran's jaw, frustration running rampant in every part of him.

"Jordan, you can't tell me that you don't feel something here. Something between us. It was there when I was sixteen—it was there after the funeral. Help me here, Jordan." God, how close was Kieran to what Jordan actually felt. Too damn close. Anger was the only defence he had.

"Don't you fucking dare! I didn't feel anything for you then, and I sure as hell don't feel anything now. Who the fuck do you think you are?"

"You kissed me when I was sixteen," Kieran offered softly, tilting his head to one side, a damn understanding expression on his face.

"It was a stupid fucking dare." Jordan wanted to hurt, his words staccato hard.

"Under the tree, after the funeral, you kissed me then."

"What?" He was incredulous. "So that kiss was somehow all *my* fault?"

"I didn't say that. I—"

"Don't put this on me. We were both there, both in the kiss, only you ran away from it all." There it was. The very crux of the whole thing, the single point that Jordan wanted to make, temper softening to sadness on the turn of a sigh.

"I went back to London, to my work, to what was real for me. I didn't run." Kieran touched him again, his hands soft with entreaty, his eyes wide.

"You ran. *You're* the one who left me here. Kieran, it didn't matter what happened, whether it was wrong or right. Above it all, you were my friend, and you left me here to—" Jordan's heart was beating faster in his chest, temper there again, and grief climbing steadily in him, his stomach in knots. "You left me there after the funeral. You went away to *heal yourself,*" Jordan injected so much sarcasm into those two words he could almost taste the bitterness of them.

"I had just lost my brother." Kieran sounded suddenly so confused.

"And I lost the man I loved," Jordan snapped brutally. "But I stayed. Alone. And tried to patch the hole that you tore in your family when you took off."

"I couldn't stay." Desperation bled into Kieran's words. He slid his hand up Jordan's chest, bowing his head. "My brother wasn't dead a week and I was lusting after you like some dog in heat."

"Kieran—"

Kieran looked back up. "Why are you so damn pretty? Why did you do that to me?"

"Don't you *dare* lay this all on me," Jordan snapped, and Kieran looked alternately horrified and regretful.

"I'm sorry, I didn't mean that you— J, it wasn't your fault."

"You left of your own accord. Don't even think of saying it was me that made you go."

"I was no good to my family then. Please. I was no good to you. God, you say it like I even had a choice in whether to stay."

"Kieran, grow the fuck up. You had a choice." Jordan felt the frustration of temper clouding his ability to string sentences together, pain in him like he'd never felt before. "You *always* had a choice. And you *know* that. You knew it then, but you couldn't do it. You left me, man. You left me to deal with Brad's death, with the mess you made of your parents' love for you, the business, *everything!*" Jordan's breathing tightened as the realisation of exactly what he'd been doing over the previous years came crashing down on him. "You left me alone. You held me at the grave, under our tree. You promised it would all be okay. And then— You. Left. Me. Alone." His voice faltered, and he stood silently, head bowed. "Alone." The word was damning.

"But—" Kieran sounded stunned. "No. You weren't alone, Jordan. You had a life here, a good life, something I had no right to destroy."

The words washed over Jordan, and he shuddered. When he looked up, the fury in him rivalled the pain and, for the moment, won out. "Is that what you said to convince yourself that you were doing the right damned thing? Is it? That I wouldn't be alone? Answer me, Kieran."

"T-they told me," Kieran stuttered. "M-mom said she would look after you."

"She's your mother, and you didn't even slow down long enough to make sure that your parents could handle Brad's death, let alone watch me? You deserted them. Your mom and dad loved you! They wouldn't do anything to stop you if you truly felt that leaving was the only option. And they would never, and I mean *never*, have told you to come back. All they ever wanted was for you to have the life you were looking for."

"I was trying to make things right. I promise you that." Kieran removed his hand from where it had rested on Jordan's arm.

"They *did* look after me as much as they could. Kieran," Jordan's voice softened, more from weariness than anything, "they're great people. I would have been as stupid as you were if I'd left them like you did."

"You could have left."

"I didn't want to leave. At first I stayed working for the company out of guilt for what happened to Brad. But I never left because of your folks, and because their hopes became part of mine." He heard the resolution in his own voice, watched as Kieran winced.

"You were like a son to them. I know."

"I know," he said, and his voice toughened again, "and I worked because I loved it, and I work for AC because I love your folks. But it never filled the hole…"

"That Brad left?" Kieran sounded so damn understanding, injecting that tone of patient calm into his voice that Jordan hated.

"No. That *you* left this family when you ran."

"Jordan—"

"No. I'm done talking, Kieran."

"Jordan," he repeated seriously. "Please let me have a

turn to talk. Just two minutes."

"Two." Jordan had already begun to repair his barriers, knowing that whatever Kieran said would be too much for him to hear.

"I'm not the same person who ran to London."

"Bullshit, Kieran—" Jordan couldn't—no, didn't control the temper that simmered through his voice, but Kieran carried on, not flinching away despite Jordan's obvious anger. If they kept talking, everything was going to come out—Jordan could feel it. Kieran would learn the truth that Brad had fallen out of love with Jordan, how they had argued, how much the older brother had resented the younger.

"No. Listen to me. I can't make excuses for the choices I made when I was younger. I ran then because there was every chance I could fuck everything up between me and Brad."

"You were just a kid, Kieran."

"Shit, Jordan, I knew how I felt. I loved you. I loved my brother's boyfriend so much it hurt." Kieran's eyes held bright conviction. It sent a shiver down Jordan's spine, and his resolve to remain angry began to waver. "You were my brother's lover, but I wanted you more than I wanted my next breath. That kiss on my birthday… I had thoughts in my head that made no sense. I wanted more, and I couldn't have it." He pressed long fingers against his temples, rubbing at the skin there as if he could press the memories from his head. "I know I was only a kid, but I wasn't blind. I saw how you were together. Sometimes it was like the two of you being together was the easy option. I could have loved you better than that, Jordan. I *did* love you."

Jordan winced—he hadn't realised other people had seen just how up and down his relationship with Brad was, or that a young Kieran had been that perceptive.

"When Brad died, when I came back home for his funeral"—Kieran's breath hitched, and Jordan could see distress in his eyes—"I saw you, and it was like I had never

100

left." He paused, his eyes bright, a hand laid over his own chest, clenched over his heart. "Don't you think I had regrets at what I did, at how I totally lost it? I betrayed my own brother who hadn't even been dead for a week." Self-hatred dripped from Kieran's voice, and he was shaking his head at the horror he obviously felt at his actions.

"It wasn't just you," Jordan admitted carefully. His temper was changing subtly, crossing over to concern at the naked pain in Kieran's voice.

"Jordan, I can't ever apologise for what happened. There is nothing I can do or say now that will ever make what happened after the funeral right."

Jordan was confused. To his ears, it sounded as if every word he stumbled over was new to Kieran. Kieran may have harboured the thought that he could explain away what had happened, but trying to do so had shown him that he actually couldn't.

"I can only beg for another chance to wipe the slate clean. I won't touch you again — I can do that. I can try not to love you."

Jordan's defences shattered completely. "You can't stop. I can't stop."

"Jordan, please —" Kieran stopped speaking, clearly not sure what to say.

Cautiously, Jordan took a single step closer and looked up at Kieran.

Motionless, because the fear and uncertainty in Kieran's eyes forbade any sudden movement, Jordan waited. Fingers trembling, Jordan touched Kieran's jaw line like a blind man learning a new face. Delicately, he traced Kieran's jaw and cheeks, then slid his fingers up over the bridge of his nose and across his forehead. Learning. Eyes shut. Looking into what he touched the way he looked into a new piece of wood he planned to carve. Seeking something. Kieran was barely breathing.

"If you touch me — please — just don't." Kieran's voice was little more than a whisper.

A faltering step and Jordan opened his eyes and brought his hands down to rest on Kieran's forearms. Another half step and he leaned towards Kieran. Lips barely touching Kieran's, he kissed him. He felt Kieran startle at the touch, and he tilted his head to deepen the kiss and to relax against Kieran.

The memories of other kisses were there. The tenderness and the need, and every emotion they had spent so long trying to hide flooded into the touch. Kieran pulled him even closer, and Jordan didn't even think to stop. The kiss deepened, and he couldn't get close enough. The taste of Kieran was so familiar from his brilliant live memories, and so different from Brad. Kieran took his time to map every inch of his mouth, his hands moving from neck to hair and back to the base of his spine. He couldn't get enough. It was right, it was real, and suddenly he let everything go. All the pain and the regret and the sadness. It was enough to let himself sink into Kieran's need.

The night was silent about them, and every single nerve ending was aware of Kieran's touch. Finally, they were sharing. Finally, they could maybe show each other what they had hidden. So many things to talk about, so much to clear. But for now it was enough to taste and touch and learn.

They didn't move away from each other for a very long time.

The kissing was hot. Having Jordan in his arms, the very stuff his dreams were made of, was enough to keep him going for life. They began to talk in-between kisses. Nothing about Brad, or love, or the big picture, focusing instead on the micromanaging of the project they had agreed to undertake.

"The Johnson house has been altered so many times over the years," Jordan mused, leaning in for another kiss, just a mere brush of lips, punctuation to every sentence. "It's going to be hard to separate the original features from the later additions."

Kieran loved that they were talking and kissing and just being close, but it was still like a dream.

"We need to know what's worth saving." Kieran found himself saying, leaning back in for another kiss, searching for the grin—loving the grin.

It was rare to find a period house that hadn't been altered over the years, and it was always hard to know what had been added and when.

"It has this awesome fireplace," Jordan pointed out, and Kieran knew immediately that this was as good as finding gold. One of the most desirable original features to find intact in any renovation was the fireplace. They were once found in almost every room of period homes, but as these houses were modernised, they were seen as redundant and were ripped out and replaced. Jordan's palpable excitement of the history in the house was feeding Kieran's own anticipation.

They kiss-talked about accounts with local suppliers, building codes and permits, renovation grants and permitted development rights. It felt natural that Jordan was the one with the project management skills, which complemented Kieran's design skills perfectly, and the rest Kieran knew would follow. It would be the two of them in this. The two of them together on this project and maybe working on some of this other stuff as well was exciting.

"We'll need to start with general cleanup, look at the foundations and major structural problems—" Kieran stopped Jordan's words with a heated kiss, his tongue searching and tasting and his hands dropping to trace the curve of Jordan's ass.

"Uh-huh," he said softly when they parted. "Make it dry—the roof, windows, weakened walls, joists and carrying beams…"

"Fuck, Kieran," Jordan whimpered, tangling his fingers in Kieran's hair. "Wiring… We need to—"

"The well, I remember the old well." Kieran shifted

again, slightly lifting Jordan, taking his weight, his breath escaping on a gasp as the sensation of touching the man he had wanted his entire life started to filter through his guilt.

"We would need a new well pump...and a—fuck—filtration system. Kieran..." It had become a game, punctuating each sentence with a kiss.

Jordan stopped talking, gave Kieran another kiss, then he pulled his head back, kiss-biting a trail from Kieran's lips to the pulse at the base of his neck. Kieran was doing everything he could to keep control of himself. There was no freaking way he was going to lose it like some damn sixteen-year-old against his momma's house. He turned thoughts over and over in his head—blueprints, shop drawings, insulation, drywall. Having Jordan pressed so close, tasting a journey from the base of Kieran's throat back up to his lips, was enough to drive a man mad.

Smirking, Jordan pulled back. "Installing baseboards, which is something we need to consider."

"M-moulding," Kieran stammered, moving his hands, widening and strengthening his stance, until Jordan was entirely dependent on him for balance. It was a heady feeling, this needy mass of man draped against him, so damn hard. "Trim...around windows and doors." He was entirely too breathless as Jordan's hold in his hair tightened to just this side of painful.

"Bookcases... Fuck, Kieran, I missed you. We need to... The...featured coving and skirting."

"Make it beautiful," Kieran finished in a rushed gasp. The taste of Jordan was intoxicating, the subtle taste of beer so incredibly perfect, more than he could possibly have ever imagined. It was unlike anything he'd ever felt before, exhilarating, the darkness of the night closed in around them. There was nothing that could have stopped Kieran from what he did next. He was so damn close that he didn't have one shred of rational thought in him. He was going to lose it, hot and heavy in his jeans, right here, a few feet from his childhood bedroom, just like he lost it when he was sixteen and had first tasted heaven. He had to stop or he had to finish, and he was fast approaching that point when a decision wasn't even going to be possible.

Gently he eased his hold on Jordan, who whimpered at the loss of Kieran's hold, pushing back until something in Kieran must have made him see what was happening. Groaning, he seemed to accept what Kieran was trying to do. Kieran closed his eyes even as Jordan released the tangle of hair in his hands and shakily tried to take a step back.

"Can we stop?" Kieran asked carefully, clinging tight to Jordan's biceps, not wanting to release the touch. Jordan screwed his eyes tight shut, his hands resting on Kieran's chest, his breathing laboured. "This feels—"

"Wrong?" Jordan didn't sound disappointed, just somewhat resigned. Obviously expecting the worst, his smile had gone, and he looked suddenly so sad.

"Shit no, this feels very right. There's just so much in my head to process."

Jordan looked thoughtful, his head tilted to one side. He was weighing up Kieran's carefully measured words.

"Yeah, too much in here." Jordan tapped his head then smiled broadly. Leaning in the few inches that separated them, he kissed Kieran lightly then pulled back. With his full generous mouth curved into another patented Salter grin and a quirk of his eyebrow, he stepped back and turned to leave. "Later, Kieran," he threw back over his shoulder.

Kieran just smiled back weakly, watching the man he loved disappear around the corner. He slumped back against the wall, only then realising how damn cold it was in Vermont at this time of the night.

Chapter Twelve

Jordan rolled onto his side in the pool of bright light that spilled in through the slightly open drapes. He yawned widely, stretching his hands high above his head, a sleepy smile on his face.

He had only got back to his room a few hours before dawn. He and Kieran had spoken a small amount. Not any more about Brad. Not much more about the spectre that haunted them both. They spoke of the house they were renovating, excitement coursing through Jordan when he had Kieran laughing with him, inches away from dark eyes and kiss-wet lips. It was such an intense memory, indelibly imprinted on his brain, and for a few delicious moments, he replayed the events of the night before.

The clock by his bed showed it was only a little after six but there was no way he was going to get any more sleep. For the first time in years, he had a thread of optimism in him, like maybe he didn't need to worry on his own, that now he had someone to help. It was energy coursing through him, and as he pulled on jeans and yesterday's T-shirt, he knew what he wanted to do next.

When he'd got back to his room last night, he had used his hand to get himself off. It had felt almost as if doing so was some kind of freaky violation, but with the images of kissing and fumbling and holding in his head, he'd really needed something. Now, he wanted a shower in that damned shared bathroom.

He grabbed clean clothes then took the stairs three at a time, dropping with a jump to the gravel at the bottom. He grinned widely as he entered the house and saw Hayley spooning cereal into her mouth.

"Early for classes, isn't it, Hays?" he started conversationally then dropped his gaze and focused on coffee when she looked at him suspiciously. He wasn't best known for his early morning mood being that good, and he smiled inwardly at what had brought on the unheard of occurrence.

"Math lecture," she answered, forcing books into an already bulging bag, "and a pre-test." She attended a local college, two bus rides away, but close enough to not warrant accommodation away from home. It was her way of contributing to the tight family finances, not that anyone begrudged her attendance. She was there on scholarship and was scarily clever. She never mentioned the placement she had turned down at MIT, or the reasons why she had refused to spend her small trust fund on the fees. She brooked no discussion on the matter, and Jordan couldn't have loved her more. She had given up an awful lot, an almost guaranteed bright future with the country's finest young brains, just to make sure her family was settled.

"You going out with Alex tonight?" Jordan liked Alex. So far.

"Yeah. Back by midnight, after we do the drug runs." She smirked and dropped a kiss to Jordan's forehead.

"I'll be waiting with the cops." This was a long-standing joke, and it was good to have that normality in the otherwise strangeness of the new day.

Toast now held between her teeth, she exited the kitchen, shutting the door behind her, and Jordan stayed where he was for a moment, sipping on coffee and relaxing tense neck muscles. He wanted a shower, a shave, to brush his teeth, then he really needed to go find Kieran. He wanted to see the plans and sketches Kieran had made. He told himself that was all. He had no other ulterior motive.

Who was he kidding? What he really wanted was more kissing.

The bathroom was empty, and he started the shower,

waiting for the hot water to work its way through the old pipes. When the water was hot enough, he climbed in and simply revelled in the luxury of the heat on him, soaping every inch of his body until his skin nearly squeaked. His cock had been at half-mast since he'd entered the shared bathroom, the room itself smelling of the apple shampoo and woodsy shower gel that Kieran used and sending blood south as quick as he could say erection. He leant back under the water, sighing as it sluiced away the soap, and held his cock in his hands. Images from last night of Kieran holding him close and the feel of the kisses added to his own erotic imaginings of Kieran in this same shower meant he was edging before he realised. Panting with exertion, he willed himself to back off. He wasn't going to rush this.

Bringing himself off to the thought of Kieran spread naked under him, of Kieran whimpering and keening for Jordan's touch, he finally shot, hot and instant over his clenched fist with Kieran's name on his lips. The cum washed away, swirling down the drain. He allowed himself a few moments, closing his eyes and leaning against the wall of the shower, before pulling himself together and shutting off the water.

He stumbled as he saw Kieran leaning against the connecting door to his room, just staring. An eternity of emotions passed unspoken between them—want, need, apology, regret—and Jordan couldn't move.

Quietly, Kieran approached him, pulling the towel from the rail and running it down Jordan's chest, his face carefully blank. What was the younger man thinking? Had he heard Jordan whimper his name? How much had he seen?

"Kieran?" The simple name was full of meaning as Kieran released his hold on the towel. Jordan clasped it, closing his eyes then pulling back.

"Morning," Kieran half whispered, leaning forward briefly just to kiss Jordan. It was a close-mouthed kiss, nothing with the passion and lust from last night.

"M-morning," Jordan stumbled over his words, his head

spinning. What did Kieran want now? What did Kieran want to do?

"Come and see the sketches for my ideas?"

Well, that was something he hadn't expected, but it certainly dealt with the awkward discussion of what had happened against the wall in the dark or the whole jerking off in the shower thing.

"I'll be there in five." Jordan was proud of himself for at least stringing together one coherent sentence.

Kieran left, and Jordan quickly pulled on clean clothes and brushed his teeth. He caught sight of a bruising mark at the base of his throat and touched it with his fingers, unable to recall the exact moment when Kieran had marked him.

When he walked into Kieran's room, it was to sketches and drawings spread across the floor—a few of the house, but mostly sketches of people and places. Kieran waved expansively, a blush on his cheeks, his shoulders hunched. "It's my London work."

Jordan crouched on the floor, sifting through one after another of many beautiful sketches and pencil drawings, images of the city that Kieran had lived in. Businessmen with umbrellas hurrying through the rain near St Paul's Cathedral, standing stark and secure against the storm of an English day. A blue-ink sketch of a chauffeur holding open a car's door in front of Harrods, for a woman talking on her cell and clutching a small dog. The images were all of iconic structures forming the backdrop for normal everyday life. Exactly how Kieran saw architecture.

"These are gorgeous, Kieran," he said softly, looking up at him and half smiling at the pride on Kieran's face. "You're very talented."

"Thank you. You always used to say that."

"I wasn't lying then, and I'm not lying now." He turned pages over to see Canary Wharf, the tall structure against the distant and familiar London skyline, and birds circling the heights. Amazing.

Kieran pulled a folder out of a case, thick and held together with a band. Carefully he passed it to Jordan, who frowned at the sudden serious look on Kieran's face. He released the band and pulled out the sheaf of papers inside, dropping the folder to the bed. He looked at each one. Every single one was of Brad. Standing, sitting, laughing, sleeping in the yard in the sun, every single inch of him so carefully drawn.

"He was my brother." Kieran's voice was so low that Jordan had to strain to hear. "I loved him." Jordan's breath caught in his chest at the stark simplicity of Kieran's words.

"So did I," he offered in response, carefully pulling the sketches together then placing them back in the folder. He then looked back at Kieran, aware that the dread of where this conversation was heading must have been carved into his face as plain as day.

"One day we need to talk," Kieran said simply, reaching for Jordan's hand and tugging him in for a tight embrace. Jordan wasn't ready to talk. He just wanted to keep innocence of this fragile relationship a while. But yes, one day, they would need to talk. Lay the ghosts to rest.

"I know."

Chapter Thirteen

They sat on Kieran's bed, leafing through the sketches of the Johnson house.

"Are you sure we should be quoting for this renovation?" Jordan was still not entirely convinced they were doing the right thing.

"I think we're at the point where it's make or break. Don't you?"

"I guess at least you have money to back it up if we need more help."

Kieran refused to look him in the eyes, and Jordan immediately knew something wasn't quite right.

"About that." Kieran looked sheepish. "I may have just about used up all my capital to repay the back mortgage payments."

"May have?" Jordan was aware he probably sounded like a parrot, repeating what Kieran said. Kieran clearly had money—he was a successful architect. How else could he have paid off the loan?

"All of it, all I had, is gone to clear the back debt," Kieran said carefully. "I have maybe a thousand left in my account. The rest of the loan is untouched."

"Shit, Kieran." The enormity of what Kieran had just revealed was like a punch in the gut. Not so much that he had no money, more from the fact that he had cleared his savings out by repaying the back payments. "Your entire account?"

Kieran rounded on him then, his grey eyes sparking with a kind of passion that only someone like Jordan, who himself had sacrificed things to make this company work, could understand.

"I will do anything for my family," Kieran said firmly, allowing no room for discussion, and Jordan said nothing in return. What had immediately risen in his thought was *why did you stay away?* but he pushed it down, trying to leave things in the past where they should stay. Clearly Kieran had reasons to stay away, not the least of which was wanting his brother's lover.

"Okay, so what you're saying is that we're taking this on with little or no financial backup?"

"Yeah."

"So we have no way of buying materials, or pulling in contractors?"

"None."

"Shit, Kieran."

"I'm thinking we should ask the Johnson family for an advance."

"Based on what?" People didn't do that. They staggered payments, but jeez, it was the way of the world now. It was a purchaser's market and so much harder to ask for an advance instead of the traditional bond.

"Good faith?" Kieran offered gently. "He's friends with Dad. We could ask Dad if he—"

"No, we can't get your dad involved. He's not well." Jordan didn't mean to come off as rude, but Kieran hadn't seen his dad when he was really bad, when he'd had his first heart problems. Kieran shifted where he sat.

"I may have already spoken to him about it," he offered sheepishly.

Which is how Jordan found himself driving Phil and Kieran to the Johnson place for a meeting with Old Man Johnson with a sheaf of papers detailing costs and Kieran's designs. Phil had managed to convince Jordan that, despite his ill health, he should accompany them, simply because Johnson and he had been on the same softball team when they were younger.

Johnson was the same age as Phil, but looked older, years

112

of sailing making his skin like leather and a lifetime of smoking pulling and tugging at that same skin, lining him with interest.

There was a lot of exchanging of memories, but at the end of the visit, when Johnson shook Phil's hand, it was shaking on Addison Construction carrying out the renovation and with an agreed twenty per cent advance on the work.

It was only now as Phil nearly collapsed into his chair in the front room that exactly what this man had done hit Jordan. Kieran was fussing over his dad, and Jordan simply sat on the chair opposite.

"Thank you," he said steadily over the noise of Kieran fussing and Phil protesting at the fuss. Both men stopped and looked over at him, and all of a sudden, much against what he normally tried to achieve, he was once again the centre of attention.

"Thank you?" Phil's eyes narrowed, and Jordan was squirming in the seat at the thoughtful stare.

"For coming with us. I think it made all the difference to him trusting us to do the work with the money he advanced."

Phil said nothing. He opened his mouth like he wanted to say something but maybe couldn't find the words. Kieran squeezed his dad's hand and pushed himself to stand tall, probably sensing the awkward moment that existed. It wasn't Phil's company anymore. It belonged on paper to Kieran, Jordan and Hayley—the mantle had been passed.

"Make me proud," Phil finally said, "and get your sister to start learning the books. Math is what she's good at. Make her earn her share."

"We will, Dad." Kieran was earnest and looked unexpectedly, impossibly young in Jordan's eyes. Under the muscles and the height and the every-which-way scruffy blond hair, the boy that had tagged along with Brad and him still remained. He looked oddly vulnerable as he promised his dad that he would make this work, and pride filled Jordan that he was loved by this man. A sudden movement twitched in his pants, and he was already half hard, a constant state of affairs since the whole shower incident this morning.

There was something here, something Jordan thought he would never see when Kieran had left after the funeral. A connection, a physical lust and want and an ache to taste Kieran again. He had come so close to losing it last night, cloaked in the moon-thrown shadows that invited confidence. It was impossible to stop staring, and he found himself uncomfortable as Kieran caught him and smirked. God. Damn. Smirked. His cock was very interested, and his intellect wanted to know more about Kieran than fuzzy memories of summers when he was young. Mostly though, he just wanted to touch, and the intensity of this want scared him.

"I'm going to have a sleep now, boys." Phil interrupted Jordan's rambling inner monologue, and his voice was firm.

Kieran leant down to drop a kiss on his dad's head. "We're outta here," he assured his clearly exhausted dad, and Jordan nodded his agreement. Following Kieran's cue, he left the front room, pulling the door closed behind him. The rest of the house was empty. Anna was at the store, Hayley safely at school, and Jordan needed one thing. Just one damn thing. Grasping Kieran's hand, he pulled him through to the hall and up the stairs, not giving Kieran one inch to manoeuvre away or to protest. At the top of the stairs, he paused to decide which way to move, and a split second decision had him guiding them both to Kieran's room. When the door shut off the rest of the world, it was mere seconds before Jordan had his hands on the man he craved, cradling his face and pulling him down for an open, searching kiss. This need to kiss Kieran was an addiction, and Kieran was certainly getting with the program. He held Jordan closer.

After looking at Kieran's drawings this morning, there hadn't been time between that and the meeting with Johnson for any kind of talking, let alone really deep discussions.

Brad's spectre was hovering there, the elephant in the corner of the room. Jordan wasn't ready to deal yet, and he needed to be selfish. They both needed to be selfish. If they had any chance of making the slightest bit of sense of this whole mess, then he had to compartmentalise Brad and separate him from Kieran. Kieran pushed, steering him, willing and ready, towards the bed until the wooden side hit the back of his knees and he tumbled down onto the covers.

Jordan was off centre, draped half on and half off the bed. Kieran stood tall over him, then, leaning down, he placed a hand either side of Jordan's hips.

Tension had been curling in Kieran since he had walked in on Jordan in the shower. Unknown to the green-eyed man prone on the bed, he had watched him lose it over his own hand. Kieran heard his name as a curse on Jordan's lips as the man had come, hot and heavy, a look of intense ecstasy on his face. Kieran had almost come in his jeans at the sight. He didn't think he'd ever seen anything so perfect, so beautiful in his life. It had made him impossibly hard, and when he'd taken the towel from Kieran...

All he had really wanted to do at that point was to step in the shower and push Jordan against the wall and climb all over him. He had wanted Jordan since he'd been old enough to know he was gay and that his brother's best friend was sex personified. He'd wanted to taste every inch of that golden freckled skin dusted with dark hair, but he hadn't. He'd wanted to drop to his knees and worship this man that had held his heart since he'd reached puberty, but he couldn't. Brad was there in all of this, the ghost in the corner of Kieran's mind, watching everything the younger brother did. Somehow Kieran was being offered everything he'd ever wanted, everything that had been Brad's. What he'd wanted the most was lying there, *on his bed*, wanting him back. He stumbled ever so slightly as indecision battled with need.

"Kieran?" Jordan reached up to run a hand through

Kieran's hair, twisting fingers in the short length, his pull on Kieran's head insistent, until his mouth was only an inch from Jordan's.

Jordan stopped. It was visibly up to Kieran to close the distance here, his decision to make, as Jordan had clearly made his.

"What am I doing?" Kieran half whispered, lust circling in his brain, sparking his nerve endings with need. He winced as he realised what he'd said, waiting for Jordan to push him away at the apparent self-doubt.

"It's been so long for me," Jordan replied, his voice low. "How long for you?"

Kieran groaned, leaning the final breath of distance and kissing Jordan gently, then he pulled back. "Since I was with someone?"

"Not just that," Jordan whispered in reply, "but for you... How long since you have wanted this, wanted us?"

Kieran was quick to shake his head, sneaking another soft kiss. "It isn't just want for me. I thought you would know that from what I said." Reaching up, he untwisted Jordan's hand from his hair. He lay back on the bed next to Kieran. Jordan rolled to his side and propped himself up. Kieran felt those clever fingers finding the hem of his T-shirt and sneaking under the soft cotton to the skin underneath.

"Talk to me, Kieran."

"I can't think of another way to say it. I just know that I love you."

"Kieran, you can't love me, not really. Damn it, you hardly know me."

Kieran jumped in, cutting off at the pass whatever else Jordan was going to say. He didn't want to discuss this, nor did he want an *I love you too* in reply. He didn't need platitudes and empty promises. Not at this point.

"I have half loved you since I was a teenager. Hell, maybe even before that." He brought his arm up to cover his eyes, welcoming the anonymity of the darkness instead of having to focus on Jordan's knowing expression. "I wanted you," he mumbled, embarrassment staining his skin with heat. "I needed you like you would never understand. I couldn't have you because you were with Brad, and I didn't know how else to deal."

"You left."

"Twice."

"I understand, you know. More than you will ever imagine."

"But you don't love me." Jordan rolled fully until he was on his front, draped half over Kieran, his hand moving farther north and briefly sketching heat across Kieran's nipple.

"I could, Kieran. Can that be enough until we work our way through all of this?"

Jordan dropped his head until his forehead was resting in the juncture of neck and ear, his lips tracing warm breath on Kieran's skin. Kieran squirmed at the gentle touch, hard and aching, and wondering why all of a sudden thoughts were getting in the way of what he wanted.

Jordan appeared to be concentrating on his right nipple, rolling it between knowing fingers then ghosting a touch across to the other. All the while he was murmuring endearments and words of need in a low voice that was quite possibly the most erotic thing Kieran had ever heard. "I want to make you come... I want to see you lose it for me... Kieran, I know you want this as much as I do..."

The assault on his senses, the words, the smell of him, the touch of his fingers, and it was all Kieran could do to lie still. He used the hand that wasn't now trapped under Jordan to reach up and cup the back of Jordan's head, feeling the texture of the short spiky hair against his palm.

"I want to come with you." His voice was hoarse as his body finally won over the objections in his head.

"I'm here, Kieran," Jordan murmured, pushing himself up and away and grabbing at the hem of his T-shirt, twisting and pulling it up and over his head. He removed Kieran's shirt, and fumbling, they both took care of jeans and socks until they were in boxers, lying close and just touching.

Kieran was trembling as he traced a path from Jordan's nipple down to the band of his boxers, easing a finger under the snug material and touching the tip of his sex with a gentle caress. Jordan was wet, pre-cum having dampened the boxers in a small space of time, and Kieran wanted to taste.

He leaned over to capture a heated kiss, a slide of tongues, tangling, tasting, then pulled back, bringing his finger, shiny with pre-cum to his mouth and sucking it from the digit. Jordan narrowed his eyes, and Kieran felt him shift, lifting his ass off the bed in an unconscious movement of need.

"Just touching," Kieran whispered, chasing a kiss and settling in to learn the touches that sent Jordan wild. His hand located Jordan's, and he guided him to his cock. He sighed into Jordan's kiss. Kieran followed suit, and without conscious thought, they were jacking each other slowly as they kissed. The sensations were wild and Kieran couldn't imagine how he had managed to live without this—Jordan lying half under him, needy, and himself desperate for something he could only find here with the man he loved.

It evolved from kissing and gentle movements to a more frantic, messy, uncoordinated grind, and the dominant side of Kieran pushed its way to the front. With a frustrated whine, he knocked Jordan's hand out of the way, swallowing Jordan's protest with a breath-stealing exchange and tangle of tongues. He pushed at his boxers then Jordan's, replaced Jordan's hand with his own, aligning their cocks, heated and hard, in his hand, pulling them together in a slipping erotic motion. He felt his balls draw up as orgasm started to build. He knew it wouldn't be long, and he had to pull back to grab oxygen.

"Fuck—you close?" Kieran tried to push the words out, needing to know. He wanted to push Jordan over the edge, but his lover couldn't answer as he stiffened and gasped, his eyes tight shut, coming hard over Kieran's hand.

Jordan let go a muttered expletive then twisted his hand into Kieran's hair, pulling him back for more kissing, thrusting still into the tight circle of Kieran's hand, his cum slicking them, and it was enough to send Kieran hurtling over the edge. He pumped his cock, feeling the heat there, the slick of them both, and losing himself in kisses. There was so much he wanted to say. So much.

He moved gently, still attached by the lips, grabbing his T-shirt and wiping at the mix of cum on Jordan's stomach and on his own hand. Then with a sigh of regret at leaving the kiss, he scooted up the bed, tugging at Jordan, encouraging him to follow, until they were next to each other on the covers. Jordan moved in and cuddled up under Kieran's neck.

"We didn't kiss as much anymore..." Jordan half whispered. There was a layer of fear in Jordan's voice, and a tension in his body. It took a while for Jordan's words to sink through Kieran's own wandering thoughts.

"Hmm?" he managed to say, even as sleep pulled at the recesses of his mind.

"Brad." *The ghost in the room.*

"Oh." Kieran wanted to say more, but he decided he was too much of a coward to push it.

"It wasn't that kind of thing."

"Thing?"

"Towards the end...the whole relationship I had with Brad..." He paused, but Kieran didn't interrupt, aware Jordan was clearly struggling with something he needed to say. "The physical side, it wasn't happening—not with me. He didn't seem interested or...aroused...with me. Our relationship had changed. It wasn't exclusive."

Jordan turned his face and buried himself into Kieran's neck. Unconsciously, Kieran pulled him in closer, a contradiction to the rising anger in him. He hadn't known that things had been bad between Jordan and his brother. He had always imagined them to be happy together.

"Brad's idea," Jordan said sadly, his breath warm against

119

Kieran's skin. "Said we were too young to be with one person forever, said the best thing was to have an open relationship."

"Oh." Kieran didn't know what else to say. He wasn't an expert on relationships by any stretch of the imagination, but what his brother had said to Jordan seemed wrong. Well, in his opinion, it was fucked up, but then he wasn't exactly a man of the world. Evan constantly teased him about being too vanilla, and he guessed maybe his friend had been right all along.

"It wasn't me," Jordan said, interrupting his thoughts. "I didn't want it. I never went with another man. I just watched him leave the bars and took him back every time. I don't know what he did, how far he went, but I loved Brad. I just wanted him to be happy. I guess I thought he needed something else other than me." There was so much pain in Jordan's voice, such intense sadness, it was hard not to wish his brother had never touched Jordan's life at that point.

"Jordan—"

"He said he was always safe, condoms—shit, it was so fucking clinical when he told me. I didn't know how to handle it. He wanted—" Jordan stopped suddenly, as if he was about to say something else then had decided better of it.

"What did he want?" Kieran was careful to keep his tone low, encouraging confidence, carding his hand through Jordan's hair rhythmically.

"Adventure. Change. He wanted a life away from this small town, wanted to see the world, wanted freedom." Jordan paused and lifted his head, his green eyes thoughtful. "He wanted what he thought you had."

That was so wrong. Brad had had everything Kieran had ever wanted. Brad had had Jordan. Kieran said not one word of what he wanted to say.

"Did he let you know this?"

"That's what we would argue about. That last argument—

if you can even call it an argument—he was drunk... Shit."

"What argument?" Kieran was already sure in his heart that he knew, but he wanted to hear it from Jordan's kiss-swollen lips.

"In the truck. The night he died."

Kieran pulled his lower lip between his teeth, a frown on his face and so much spinning in his brain that he didn't know where to start. Jordan had levered himself up to rest on his elbows, staring at him with something akin to fear on his face and a healthy amount of resignation. There were two ways this could go, and Kieran needed to make the right decision. His brother had died feeling jealous of him. His brother had died because he was drunk, high and arguing with Jordan.

Kieran could become defensive, not understand. The shock over these new revelations was certainly pushing for answers. Or, he could see the man that was part of his life now, hurting and carrying so much guilt...

Jordan's green eyes were focused and intent, and he moved himself up and away from Kieran, evidently thinking he had completely fucked everything up now.

At the end of things, it wasn't a difficult decision for Kieran to make. They needed to talk, one day soon, but at the heart of it, Kieran knew Jordan almost better than he'd known his brother in some ways. Without hesitation, he reached for Jordan before he could go, gripping tight to his upper arms.

"Do you really think that the argument caused the accident?" It was a simple question, and one Kieran already knew the answer to from the forensic evidence that had been passed to him by his dad. He just wanted Jordan to see what had really happened and to somehow start to let it go.

"No, he took his belt off... He wanted to... We hit a—"

Kieran pulled him in for a kiss, stopping his words with a long, lazy kiss, tongues tangling and breaths exchanged. Kieran finally pulled back, releasing his grip on Jordan and encouraging him to lie back down against him.

"Sometimes I miss him so much it hurts," Kieran said simply. Jordan burrowed deeper into his grip then mumbled something against Kieran's chest, so low Kieran had to strain to hear. "What?"

Jordan sighed and lifted his head. "I'm sorry you lost him."

"It wasn't your fault. None of it was your fault."

"Absolving me with words is all well and good, but it doesn't change that I blame myself. Don't get me wrong..." He paused, and sighed. "I'm glad you don't blame me, and I'm glad your family doesn't blame me." Jordan was obviously struggling with this topic, and Kieran wasn't entirely sure what he should be doing, but it seemed that maybe changing the subject would be good for both of them.

"Let's get this house done, okay? Then I promise you we'll work through the rest of it as we go."

Chapter Fourteen

"So, the thirty dollars for that was carried over from the first month and goes in the credit column." Hayley was showing Kieran the statement reconciliation, whizzing through numbers like everyone knew tax was at a certain percentage over a certain amount. Like it was easy and simple to understand. He had followed most of it, but this whole creditor-debtor crap was really making his head spin. He was so determined to become more than just someone who worked at AC. He wanted to know it all, but he wondered if maybe accounting was a step too far.

"Why in the credit column? Surely it's a debit to us."

"Because we owe them — they are our creditors."

"That doesn't make sense."

"Kieran," she said, sighing with exaggerated patience, "it makes perfect sense."

"I give up." He sat back in the chair. "I am never going to get this. Dad was right. You should do all the books on your own and make some use of that freaky math brain of yours."

"I don't really want you anywhere near the accounts. I'm not sure why you even wanted me to show you."

"Er, because someone else in the family needs to know how to do this just in case?" He shrugged.

"Our neighbour's six-year-old daughter could do better than you when it comes to the accounts."

"Brat." He ruffled her hair affectionately and slid the books towards her, grinning at the mix of affront and resignation in her expression. He replaced the coffee in her cup with fresh brew, then sat back down next to her and watched her concentrate. She hummed as she worked, and it reminded him of when she was five or so and she would hum as she read *Cat in the Hat* to herself.

Spontaneously, he leaned over and hugged her, earning a squeak for his troubles.

"I missed you, Hays," he said into her hair, gripping tighter as she snuggled into his embrace.

"I missed you too," was her reply. Her arms rose to wrap around him. "So much."

* * * *

The first day at the house was both exhilarating and frightening. Day one was the roof, which spread to day three, and segued nicely into windows. At this point, it was about making the house watertight, and as much as it pained Jordan, they couldn't stop to work on each window like he wanted. They really needed a strong base to build on.

"Think it'll pass?" Kieran examined each window with worry carved into his brow. Oddly enough, for the first time ever, Jordan was not worried about the level one house inspection. He knew they'd done enough to make it watertight and sound. He traced his fingers over the aged wood that remained, the parts that had been saved melding imperceptibly with the new, the smell of varnish and paint a fragrance that comforted him.

"She'll pass this stage," he said confidently.

The meeting with the inspector had gone well, the structural engineer confirming the house was solid, and it was finally on day seven that they could begin.

As for their growing relationship—by mutual, but unspoken agreement, they kept it at kissing and hugging, neither of them ready to take it any further. Exhaustion made the non-verbal accord easy to keep. It was when the weather turned, summer heat starting to show its face, that things started to get difficult, at least in Jordan's point of view. It was all due to the T-shirt that Kieran chose to wear — white, sleeveless, fitted, and clearly having seen better days. It proclaimed '*If time and space are curved, where do all the straight people come from?*' The material clung to every single muscle, and God, what a body. The sun was burnishing his skin to a healthy brown, different from his London pallor, and whenever Kieran lifted or pushed or in fact did anything at all, the defined muscles in his arms would set off a chain reaction in Jordan's body that defied explanation.

Kieran was tall like Brad — admittedly not quite as tall, six-one, not six-three — but where Brad had been lean and sculptured, smooth and his hair always perfectly so, Kieran had an edge to him. He wore his unkempt shaggy blond hair pushed back from his face with a bandana, and he wasn't scared of hard work. His skin had a perpetual sheen of sweat from hard work, and he was usually covered in dust from head to foot. Jordan knew he looked just as work weary, but crafting alongside Kieran gave him an edge, adding enthusiasm that went beyond a need to work and centred on the love he had for making things beautiful.

As they worked, stripping back orange paint and seventies wallpaper, the beauty of the old house could be more imagined. They worked from Kieran's schedule. It gelled, and by the end of week two, they had slipped into a comfortable working routine. The need for each other had changed some from the immediate hunger and need of their first meetings to the casually exchanged kisses that promised more but kept the edge off the immediate lust.

"I think we should have tonight off," Jordan suggested. They slid down the wall and leant back against the now bare hallway walls, drinking water and taking the break that had been three hours in the making.

"The whole night?" Kieran smiled and bumped shoulders with him, Jordan letting out a low laugh.

"Instead of getting it delivered, we could collect the cornicing from the city. Maybe drive up tonight then gather the stuff tomorrow first thing, get back early enough to put some work in." Jordan knew what he was saying was common sense, but he ended up frowning at Kieran's next words.

"So we are planning on booking a motel just for picking up supplies for the house?" Kieran smirked, which belied the casual question that his sentence contained. Jordan didn't even think. He placed his water on the floor and twisted himself to climb and settle astride Kieran's thighs. He thrust himself forward, just once, knowing Kieran would feel him hard in his pants, hard since the idea of sharing a night away with Kieran had come to mind. Kieran keened at the touch, pushing back, his eyes closing. Jordan leaned in to whisper in his ear.

"I was thinking, if we got there at nine, I could spend a couple of hours tasting every part of you, push you down on the bed, get you nearly there, maybe suck you off and make you lose yourself in my mouth."

"Fuck, Jordan, you keep talking, and I'm going to come in my pants." Kieran breathed, twisting his fingers in Jordan's short hair and pulling him closer for another heated kiss — more of a tongue-fuck actually, strong, determined. Jordan could feel Kieran hard and ready against him. Carefully he pushed himself away. He was not going to let their first real time be in this house. It was wrong, despite the fact that, at that moment, all he wanted was for Kieran to bend him over the nearest surface and take him high.

"We stop at five," he breathed, pushing Kieran away even as Kieran was chasing him for another kiss.

"Five" was all Kieran replied, pressing a hand against his cock and banging his head against the wall.

"Poor Kieran." Jordan smirked, getting to his feet and offering a hand to help. Kieran took the hand and in the blink of an eye, he had swapped their positions. Jordan was pressed up against the wall, trapped by Kieran's unforgiving hold, his hands gripped and pressed high above his head. They said nothing. Green eyes locked on grey, and the air hung still and silent around them. Kieran swivelled his hips, brushing his erection against Jordan in a deliberate press, using his teeth to bite a gentle mark on Jordan's bared neck. Jordan was lost in that he was pinned against the wall and that Kieran was hard and needy against him with a promise of what they could have. Casually, Kieran released his hold, stepping away with a smirk. It was Jordan's turn to whine his protest.

"Five then," he said simply, and, whistling tunelessly, he grabbed his tool belt and wandered down the hall towards the kitchen. Jordan stood for a good thirty seconds, in awe at how Kieran had turned the tables so damn fast and how it was now him needy and freaking begging for more.

"Asshole," he finally called after the retreating man, who simply waved a hand in dismissal and threw back a grin.

Bastard.

* * * *

It wasn't an expensive room. Budgets didn't allow for a hotel, but the side-of-the-road motel was as good as anything, and it provided a bed and, most importantly, privacy. They made it there just after nine, grabbing drive-through halfway on the journey and stocking up with beer and snacks at Kieran's insistence. Jordan wasn't entirely sure that food or beer was anywhere on his to-do list for tonight. He didn't say anything, though, just handed over the credit card and nodded as Kieran listed the pros and cons of an empty stomach and possible dehydration.

He called first dibs on the vaguely pitiable shower, lathering soap and cleaning his body from top to toe, going back into the main room and inclining his head to indicate it was Kieran's turn. Kieran didn't argue, and he was in and out of the shower in five minutes, his hair slicked back and his face clean of stubble, a towel wrapped around his waist, his skin glistening with water droplets.

Suddenly it was awkward.

"I guess you should know I haven't actually been with anyone since Brad." Jordan knew there was embarrassment in his voice, and he flinched at the pathetic sound in the words.

"No one?" Kieran didn't seem shocked. His tone was more possessive than disbelieving or questioning. He approached the bed and climbed on to it to balance on his knees, pulling away the towel and sitting back on his heels. He was already hard, and he closed his hand around his cock, running the length of it. "Do you know how hot that is?"

Jordan had pulled on boxers, and he didn't hesitate to slip them off and join his new lover on the bed.

"Jeez, enough with the porn talk, Addison."

Kieran feigned hurt, which quickly change to a sigh when Jordan pushed his hand away and Jordan felt the weight of him. "I'm just saying take it easy." Kieran circled his hips, eyes closing at the slide against Jordan's hold.

"Slow…easy," Kieran whispered, his hands tracing a path down Jordan's chest and to the sides, settling on Jordan's hips.

Jordan tilted his head to kiss Kieran and just enjoyed the lazy slide of tongue across his. He still moved his hand, setting a steady rhythm as Kieran pulled back and kissed a path from lips to throat. He wasn't sure how much time passed. It was like everything he'd ever wanted was here for him to take, and when Kieran said he was going to take it slow, he wasn't joking.

Jordan chased the space that separated them and pulled at Kieran's lower lip with his teeth before tasting where he had touched with his tongue. Jordan slanted his head to one side, opening to Kieran's kisses. There was nothing hard about the kisses, just a soft pressure and a gentle touch.

Jordan stopped, pulling back slightly, his face flushed, his cock hard and heavy against Kieran. "There isn't room for Brad in this bed as well, K. Are you sure about this?"

"I promise. He's not in my head, not in this room with

us," Kieran responded softly, and Jordan supported him back on the bed as gently as if he weighed nothing. Jordan wanted to make Kieran feel special, wanted, cherished. It was a feeling so hot inside him it sparked under his skin, and he nearly whimpered into Kieran's mouth.

He slid up the bed, using his elbows and feet to move, until he was lying half on and half off Kieran, his hands ghosting across the muscles of his chest and across his arms.

"I love you both ways, you know," he whispered against Kieran's heated skin. "I loved you before, all legs and arms and boyish charm, slim and sweet and boy-next-door sexy, and I love you built like this, so fucking hard and strong." He trailed kisses across Kieran's chest, biting and sucking at each nipple, focusing his teeth and his tongue on the sensitive skin, his fingers following, pulling and feeling Kieran writhe under him. He gripped Kieran's arms, feeling muscles bunching and releasing under his tanned skin, and the feel of him was like a drug. He wanted to taste, wanted to touch, but he didn't want to move. Kieran was pinned to the bed under him, and jeez, was that hot. His lover's ineffectual movements pushed his cock up against Jordan's and the painfully sharp pressure made him gasp. His own body moved in rhythm with the pace he was setting. He moved lower, biting each hard plane, each dip in the skin, marking Kieran's hip where the golden skin lay taut. Then, sucking gently, he moved his other hand down from the chest, his lips inches from where he wanted them to be.

Kieran's muscles flexed under him as he concentrated on kiss-biting a path of marks to each nipple and only stopping when Jordan decided enough was enough. Releasing his hold on Kieran, he reached to where he'd dropped supplies then dropped his hand. For a single instant, he caught Kieran's gaze, wondering how this was going to work. Jordan wasn't averse to switching it up. A wealth of information was exchanged in that single glance, and the depth of emotion in Kieran's eyes would have been frightening if Jordan didn't know him so well. Kieran wanted him.

"Shit, this is awkward," he finally said, resting his forehead against Kieran's.

Kieran tried to hold back the laugh. He was clearly trying, but finally it was too much. Kieran let his head fall back to the pillows, his hands pinned, his legs caught between Jordan's and started to laugh again.

Jordan struggled not to join in, but Kieran's laugh was so damn infectious, like a kid's giggle, and instead he focused on the fact that Kieran throwing his head back meant that his neck was exposed. Laid bare, from throat to lips, and like some compelling force, Jordan lowered his mouth and started to taste. He concentrated on the pulse at the base of Kieran's throat, feeling it flutter against his cool lips, darting out his tongue and tasting the taut skin. He listened as Kieran's laughter turned slowly to soft whimpers and his name. Jordan started to explore higher, kissing a path up the side of Kieran's neck, shifting his body slightly as his cock pushed against Kieran's hard hip bone, so fucking turned on for this man imprisoned under him.

Kieran was hot against him, and Jordan moved subtly, pushing his own cock against the younger man's, reaching up to take Kieran's groan with an open-mouthed kiss. He swallowed his name from open lips, tongues meeting, tasting, hard and insistent. Then he slanted his head to deepen the kiss, releasing Kieran's hands only to feel them instantly move to dig deep into his hair, pulling and twisting into the softness, as Kieran arched up into the kiss. Jordan heard himself groan, pushing up and away slightly, not taking his lips from Kieran's, just reaching between them to palm his own cock. It was explosive as Kieran groaned and whimpered into Jordan's mouth, wrenching his lips away — one word..."*please*"...the sound caught somewhere between a plea and a demand.

Jordan didn't hesitate, didn't argue. He pulled their cocks together in one hand — hot, heavy — twisting and capturing Kieran's mouth in a kiss that stole his own ability to catch a real breath. They moved unevenly, desperate, intent on only one thing. A singular twist of Kieran's hips against Jordan's hand, and he was lost, shouting his completion and coming so fucking strong he smacked his head back on the mattress. Jordan felt the tension, the iron grip, the release, the heat, the intensity of Kieran's bliss and fell over the edge himself, hot against the writhing man.

They stayed still, breathing heavily. Neither moved at first to break the hold that the intensity of the experience had created. Jordan lifted his arms and wrapped them around Kieran, his eyes heavy with sleep. He always felt this way after coming, wiped out, wanting to cuddle. Brad hadn't been a great cuddler, not even before the arguments when they still made love. But Kieran was all hands, manoeuvring them until he was spooning Jordan from behind. It was in that position that they slept.

* * * *

It was intense dark, absolute dark when Jordan woke to Kieran moving beside him, trailing kisses with, it seemed, only one destination in mind.

Jordan didn't stop to question what was happening. He just went with the flow, and he was completely fine until his lover decided to turn intimate attention to his cock. Kieran drew the tip into his mouth, tasting and curling, and it was difficult for Jordan not to lose it there and then when he felt Kieran's slicked fingers reaching behind.

Each small push of his finger was accompanied by kisses on Jordan's inner thighs, travelling upwards and kissing his hip bones, all the time keeping up a litany of words, encouragement, then taking his hard cock into his mouth and sucking him almost all the way to the base.

He twisted and stroked, his free hand gripping Jordan's cock, the movements slow and nowhere near enough to get Jordan off. Every so often Jordan felt Kieran's mouth on him, and it seemed as if the room, the burning of the fingers and the exquisite pleasure-pain were his only points of focus.

Kieran crooked his fingers, touching Jordan's sweet spot so softly, so gently, too fucking much. Every so often, he would add more lube, sliding his fingers out almost to the tips then pushing back in, so very slow.

"Nuh—" Jordan couldn't form words, couldn't control his breathing, waves of pleasure leaving a sheen of sweat on his skin.

"I love you, Jordan. I can't believe I have you here, under me, so fucking close just with my mouth and my fingers."

Jordan couldn't stop himself arching off the bed, his shoulders and heels the only things touching the sheets. He needed to touch Kieran, wanted to force him to push inside.

"Do you wanna come just with my fingers?" Kieran asked softly as Jordan couldn't stop himself from forcing himself down on Kieran's clever fingers. "Shall I let you come here?

"You—inside."

"Jordan, so fucking gorgeous." He pulled his fingers out, rolling the condom on as quickly as he could with slippery, slick fingers and pressing against his entrance. Instinctively, Jordan rolled to one side, and Kieran slotted himself in the position he had slept in, curled tight and protective around him. Jordan closed his eyes and visualised the pain of the burn, relaxing as much as he could. Kieran pushed forward, and Jordan swallowed the gasp. Kieran was balls deep so quickly and waiting on Jordan to move. It was different. It didn't burn so much. Kieran had clearly made sure Jordan was stretched and ready, and instead of any discomfort, Jordan just felt full and ready to move.

The rhythm was agonisingly slow, and even though Jordan tried to lead, it was very definitely Kieran who was setting the pace again—slow, steady, deep—and with so many kisses, Kieran obviously didn't want to lose that connection. Orgasm started to build to the point where Jordan knew he wasn't going to last much longer, and he breathed a warning.

"Kieran—"

"I love you, Jordan!" Kieran half shouted.

"I—" was all Jordan could say, was all that he could rationally pull together as an intense orgasm shook his body, and Kieran came inside him. Whatever was behind them, whatever had happened in the past, right here, right now, he didn't think he'd ever loved anyone any more than he loved Kieran. He just had to say it.

Closing his eyes, he rolled closer to Kieran. Ignoring the wet cum on his stomach and the satisfying ache in his ass, he prepared to say it. It was only three words—three little words.

Three words that would change his and Kieran's life forever.

Utterly determined, he opened his eyes, startled to see Kieran looking at him. It pushed him off his train of thought as Kieran collected another kiss, nothing more than a soft touch of lips, and repeated "I love you" in a soft voice. Jordan knew then exactly what he should say in return.

"I love you, Kieran James Addison."

Kieran smiled. "I know you do."

Chapter Fifteen

Jordan stretched in the bed, the soft cotton of worn sheets sliding across his heat-sensitive skin, and an intense pleasure still flowing in every pore. He meant every syllable of his "I love you," admitting inside he had always wanted to taste the younger Addison and pushing back the insistent guilt that he would probably always have. Next to him, Kieran sprawled loose limbed and smiling, and in a smooth move, Jordan turned and draped himself across his lover's broad chest.

"Hey," he whispered softly, kissing first at the smile then higher on his cheekbones.

"Tickles." Kieran squirmed as Jordan laid butterfly touches on his skin, his eyelashes sweeping across the warm tones. "Girly," Kieran murmured, and Jordan knew exactly what was coming next. It was the same thing his friends used to say at school — '*Your eyelashes are so girly. Do you have mascara on?*'

"You love it," Jordan whispered, trailing his mouth with soft open-mouthed kisses across Kieran's face and down to his throat.

"I love you," Kieran insisted, "despite your girly lashes."

It was an excuse for Jordan's kisses to turn into nips, and Kieran yelped on a laugh as Jordan decided tickling would be a good thing at that moment. It ended in an all-out war because turnabout was fair play, and despite Kieran being slightly taller and heavier, it was Jordan who seemed to have the upper hand.

"Uncle," Kieran called, his breath catching as he twisted one last time and managed to roll onto his side and away from Jordan.

For his part, Jordan couldn't stop laughing—he hadn't laughed so hard in years—until he saw them. He stilled, stopped tickling suddenly, wondered how he hadn't noticed them before. Kieran obviously felt the change and looked back at Jordan with a question on his face, which quickly turned into a frown as he clearly realised what Jordan was looking at.

Jordan didn't say anything at first, just traced the scars—three lines, two small and perfectly straight, dissecting a longer more ragged, random line that started at Kieran's lower back and curved around one hip. How had missed these? He felt them again. They weren't raised at all. He would never have known that they were there had he not actually been looking at them, and given everything they had done so far had been in the dark...

"Kieran?" It was an awful lot of questions in one word. *Why are there two scars across the base of your spine? Where is this other scar from? When were you hurt?*

"I had to have an operation a while back," Kieran started carefully, and Jordan's eyes narrowed.

"When? What for?"

"When I went back after...the second time I left. It was an onsite work review with the rest of the team, my first out of office assignment for Dewitt-Nate. There was a scaffolding collapse, and I was in the wrong place at the wrong time."

"Shit, Kieran, why didn't I know about this?" Jordan fell back against his pillow, wondering if he had either been so buried in grief over losing Brad, or whether he had been truly oblivious to things happening in his surrogate family. It hurt that he hadn't known, hurt that he hadn't been able to do something. "No one ever said anything."

Kieran rolled onto his back next to Jordan, both focusing on the same cream ceiling, and reached down to grab at Jordan's hand tightly.

"I didn't tell them, not even Hayley."

"Why wouldn't you tell them?"

135

Kieran sighed. "I was thousands of miles away. They'd lost their first son not long before… What were any of them going to do? I couldn't expect Mom, or Hayley, or anyone, to come sit by my bed for eight weeks."

In a flurry of movement, Jordan leaned up and over Kieran, his own fingers digging into Kieran's hand that gripped his so tight.

"Eight weeks? What the fuck, Kieran?"

"Coulda been out earlier, but they handed down the usual highly melodramatic bullshit—worried about the spine and not walking—but it was fine."

"Your spine?" Jordan couldn't believe what he was hearing. Kieran had been in England, alone, in a hospital for eight weeks with a spinal injury?

"Well, they went in, did some stuff." He waved his free hand expansively. "Screwed bits, added metal, untwisted stuff, and within four months, I was walking again."

"Walking? Fuck."

"I had Evan—he was there for me."

Jordan snorted at that, but didn't say anything against the man who had obviously had Kieran's back when he was ill. He had heard enough, and closing his eyes, he dropped his head to Kieran's chest, his breathing as steady as he could make it. What part of it made his stomach churn? It had happened, but now Kieran was fine. *Wait*. He was okay now, wasn't he? He lifted his head, his eyes meeting Kieran's, and it was as if Kieran knew what he was going to ask.

"Apart from carrying a letter on flights with me so that I don't set off the detectors, I am fine, I promise you. I did all the physical therapy they wanted, and I take anti-inflammatory pills if I get any pain. I get the odd panic attack every so often, like a mild claustrophobia, I guess."

"Should you be working on the house?" Jordan knew he sounded worried, but he couldn't help it. If Kieran was just doing this in a heroic effort for his family then he damn well wanted him to stop.

Kieran smiled, and his chest moved in a huff of a laugh. "I'm fine, honest."

Jordan grumbled and placed his head back on his boyfriend's chest, relishing the warmth of his skin, and feeling his cock twitch. Hell, being this close to Kieran was making him act like he was eighteen again. They lay still for a while, Kieran closing his free hand around Jordan's back and pulling him in for a closer embrace. His breathing settled into a gentle rhythm as sleep took him under.

Held against the warm skin, Jordan was being lulled into his own sleep, but images of what Kieran had gone through on his own tumbled through his head, and an unreasonable fear built inside him. It was ridiculous. One of the Addisons could have gone to England. Yes, money was tight, but Kieran should have had someone else. He thought back to when Kieran had first left, to the emptiness in the house. Phil had been quiet, but resolved, Anna had cried a few times. Hayley said it was no different than normal and was well into emailing as soon as she could. As for himself, well, he'd been relieved that he wouldn't be reminded of the kiss. That first Christmas —

"Kieran..." He lifted his head and shook his dozing lover awake. "Kieran!"

"Muh?" Kieran's reply was less than coherent, and he was blinking away sleep.

"That was the Christmas they said they wanted you to come home, the first Christmas after Brad died. You said you were too busy. You lied."

Jordan remembered it so clearly, walking in on a crying Anna, a glass of wine in front of her and the phone on the table in front of her. When Jordan had asked what was wrong, all she'd said was that Kieran wasn't coming home, that he was busy. Jordan had tried to console her. Kieran's calls had become less and less over the previous month, trickling down to just two that last week. Jordan had tried to make her see Kieran was young, that he had his own demons in losing his brother, but she'd had her own opinions.

"Yeah, I remember," Kieran replied cautiously, an uncertain expression on his face.

"She said you were drunk."

"Who?"

"Your mom, when you phoned, she said you sounded off to her and that you were drunk."

"I wasn't drunk. It was the day they said I might struggle to walk. It was a bad day. I was high on pain meds. You wouldn't believe how I needed them."

"Promise me something, Kieran?"

"Sure." Kieran didn't hesitate, obviously trusting Jordan not to get him to promise to jump off a bridge.

"Tell them. All of them. What happened to you explains a lot of missed calls and emails you didn't reply to, the seeming silence. It hurt your mom and your dad."

"It was the right decision to make at the time." Stubborn to the end was Kieran Addison.

"Yeah, I know that's what you think," Jordan readily admitted. "It was right for *you*. At the time. Now they need to know their son for who he is, not who they thought he had possibly become. They had Brad as a model. He was drinking heavily at the end but never at home. They thought you were just becoming like your brother."

"Is that what you thought?"

Jordan hesitated. He had to be truthful here. They had promised before—no lies, no untruths. "It made me cross and sad." He shut his eyes tight, not wanting to see disappointment in Kieran's eyes. Instead, Kieran pulled him even closer, every inch skin to skin.

"That's okay," he began, stroking Jordan's skin, "but we are getting past that, right?" There was hope in Kieran's voice, and a small amount of fear. Jordan snuggled and inhaled the scent of his lover, suddenly at peace.

"More than getting past it, Kieran."

Chapter Sixteen

Kieran had insisted Jordan go with him to pick Evan up from the airport. It had been a short battle, but heated.

"I don't like the guy," Jordan had snapped when Kieran had poked and prodded and pushed to know why Jordan didn't want to go.

"Okay, I get he is a bit of an idiot sometimes, but he's my friend."

"Some friend. What about bailing you out of jail for joyriding the day after your sixteenth? Calling me fairy, and shit, the alleged sex video he circulated at school of me and Brad?"

"He was a kid—I was a kid. He knew you wouldn't pound on him for calling you fairy 'cause you were older and he was my friend. He was teasing you is all, and the jail thing?" Kieran had hesitated. "That was mostly me."

"Yeah, right, *you* stole a car."

"I didn't technically steal it. It was Brad's. I had the keys, and I just borrowed it."

"Shit, Kieran. Whatever. He's always been a fucking pain in my ass," Jordan had finished then visibly deflated. Kieran had pressed in for the attack.

"He was there for me in England. I used to tell him everything, and he knows about you, about how I felt, why I stayed away. Can you not just get past this?" Kieran had been worried. It was important that his lover and his friend got along.

"Now that he's big enough to hit, if he calls me fairy…"

The threat had been unspoken, but at least Jordan was now standing next to him at arrivals, his arms crossed and his mouth pressed in a thin line.

It had been fourteen days, and despite the little fucker texting pictures of naked women daily, Kieran was so damn excited to see Evan. He had so much to tell him. He was bouncing on the balls of his feet, and not even stern Jordan could quell the enthusiasm he had. He spotted the short, spiky-haired redhead. He wasn't easy to miss. Kieran set up a mad wave, called his name, and Evan half jogged over. His smaller frame was instantly engulfed in a patented full-on Kieran-hug, with much back-slapping and quickly exchanged reports about the flight.

Kieran pulled back and half pushed Evan away, grinning down at the shorter man, at the smile in his deep brown eyes. He looked at the one case and one bag that Evan was pulling along. "Where's all your stuff?"

Something indefinable passed over Evan's face, a flicker of regret, of sadness, but it disappeared so quickly Kieran thought he had imagined it.

"This is it, Kieran," he finally said. At the same time he clearly caught sight of Jordan who, when Kieran looked, was still standing with arms folded, his face still set in stone.

Evan extended his hand with a grin. "Fair— Jordan," he said clearly, not moving his hand even though it took a good ten seconds of an assessing gaze before Jordan accepted the handshake.

"Evan," he said simply, then followed them. Kieran highly aware that Evan had his arm around him and was unintentionally blocking out Jordan. That needed to be rectified, and Kieran stopped to grab at Jordan's hand, linking fingers and squeezing supportively. Evan stopped, and his expression bordered on comical, his mouth hanging open and his eyes wide. He looked from the joined hands, to Jordan, to Kieran and back to the hands, and Kieran really had to stop himself from laughing at the sight of a quiet and dumbfounded Evan.

Evan wrinkled his nose in that way he had before he tried to say something profound, which wasn't as often as

Kieran knew he could. Finally, Evan found his voice, and Kieran realised profound was not what they were getting at this point.

"I fucking told you! You and Jordan. Jordan and you. Holy fuck!"

Jordan sighed irritably but said nothing, and for that, Kieran was thankful. In fact, when they clambered into the truck, with Evan in the back talking a mile a minute, Kieran realised how damn proud he was of his lover.

Jordan began to thaw a bit on the journey home after seeing Evan's reaction and the conversational nuggets that Kieran served up. Evan revealed to a bemused Jordan than Kieran had revealed he'd always been gay for Jordan's ass. Kieran did try to shush his friend. There were some things he really didn't want Jordan to know just yet. Evan just smirked then settled happily into his seat in the back of the truck.

"I wanna see this house you're renovating, 'cause I'm here to help," Evan said enthusiastically.

"We don't have insurance for you," Jordan interrupted quickly, and Kieran burst into laughter at Jordan's instant reaction. He knew Evan had been joking when he'd offered to help, but there was no way Jordan could know.

"Evan, you would kill yourself, and probably us, in the space of an hour," Kieran finally said when he could catch his breath from laughing so hard, thankful that it was Jordan that was driving and not him.

"I'll just make coffee for you then, and other useful shit," Evan insisted, which just set Kieran off again.

"Coffee!" he managed to force out between snorted laughs. "The last time you made me coffee you set the coffee machine on fire. Who the fuck does that?" He twisted in his seat to see an answering grin on Evan's face. "I missed you, man."

"Yeah, yeah, whatever, homo," Evan pretend-grumped, keeping up being offended until they pulled up in front of the house.

Jordan wandered off, claiming work that conveniently needed to be done in the tangled yard, so it was up to Kieran to show his friend what they had accomplished. Kieran was proud and so damn pleased with their achievements, showing the roof and the walls and the windows that made it weather tight, the well that worked, the floors sanded to a burnished sheen. The kitchen was still in disarray with piles of original wood and new cabinets. The scent of sawdust hung in the air.

"Jordan is working in here," Kieran announced proudly as Evan checked out the refurbished wall cupboards. He was actually way more than just proud of Jordan's work with its intricate detailing in gorgeous carvings. Each cabinet was built by hand from reclaimed wood, treated and sanded, with a warm lustre.

Evan ran a careful hand over some of the carving, whistling low and nodding. "Jordan did this himself?"

"All of it. He is an artist with wood."

Evan leant back against a tall cabinet, testing it was fixed in place before he did so. "Spill," he demanded, and Kieran winced. He'd known this was coming from the minute Jordan had left him alone. What did he say?

"What do you want to know?"

"All of it."

"The regrets, the guilt, Brad?"

"You can start there if you want." Kieran opened the fridge and pulled out the last two beers, passing one to Evan and twisting the cap off his. This was definitely a beer-type conversation.

"It isn't the easiest of things," he said simply and looked at the man he called friend. "Not sure how to start this, man."

"Are you happy?" Trust Evan to cut to the heart of things, as was often his way.

"Happy? Yes, very happy."

"I won't say it doesn't worry me, K."

Kieran tilted the bottle, swallowing half of it in a few

frantic gulps. "I know you don't approve—"

"Approve? Shit, my best friend is happy with the man he's wanted ever since he knew he was freaking gay. Of course, I approve. I just wish…" He paused and took a swig of his beer, rolling the liquid around his mouth before swallowing it, undoubtedly deliberating on what he wanted to say.

"What?"

"I wish Brad wasn't in all of this." Such plain, simple words, and it was a knife to Kieran's gut so intense he bent over as he stood. The air was tight in his lungs and his throat tight, the grief stumbling through him, trying to find purchase in his body. It was only what he'd been thinking since the day he'd stepped back on US soil.

"I know. Evan…"

"Shit, Kieran, I'm fucking sorry." Evan was talking, saying things, but it was all noise in Kieran's ears. Evan pulled at his arms, finally encouraging him to stand straight, using his own smaller body as a crutch. "Sorry…sorry… I didn't mean—"

"S'okay," Kieran forced out. "I need to…sit…"

Evan helped him slide down the cabinet, and finally both men were sitting next to each other, the beer forgotten and the wounds of the past wide open between them.

"Shit. I'm sorry."

"Honestly, Ev, it's okay, I have had the same things in my head. It's— Brad is in my head, but when I'm with Jordan…"

"You don't have to—"

"I do. I do have to. When I'm with Jordan, it feels right, like Brad backs off in my head, and it's just us."

"Jesus, K, you just can't do anything simply, can you?" Evan chuckled and bumped shoulders. Kieran glanced up. It was good to get that off his chest, to tell someone that he felt inside Brad would accept what was happening. He wondered though if Evan could understand just how much Kieran had in his heart that was reserved for Jordan.

"He's mine, I'm his. I love him," Kieran finally said very

143

quietly then waited for Evan to respond, and was surprised as Evan reached a hand behind him and pulled him in for a sideways hug.

"Good, Kieran. It's all good." He pulled back, glancing around the kitchen, frowning at its obvious emptiness. "No coffee maker. Shit. Well, I can't make coffee, but I can sure go buy some. Back in five."

Evan left in a flurry of shouts as to the different types of coffee Kieran would drink, upgrading to beer as Jordan shouted his order from over in knee-high weeds.

Kieran was left in the half-finished kitchen. He sat on the floor, his eyes closed, his thoughts on his brother.

"You okay?" Jordan crouched down next to him and his voice was small and quiet. "Did he upset you? Do I need to kill him?" Kieran smiled at the seriousness of the words, a lightness in his thoughts now that he'd shared his greatest fear.

"You are just waiting for an excuse to kill him, aren't you?"

Jordan wrinkled his nose and nodded slowly. "Please. Just give me the excuse."

Kieran leaned up, kissing Jordan gently, briefly. "Love you," he murmured close to Jordan's skin.

It was good to have Evan home.

* * * *

The three men sat on the porch of the half-finished property, Kieran and Evan shooting the breeze as the night closed in around them, the heat of the sun vanishing to the horizon, and Jordan leaning back on his elbows, looking up at the sky. Kieran sat in the middle, Evan to his left. Evan was talking about how he'd left London with nothing more than his bag.

"Because after my boy here left, I kinda realised I'd done my travelling, and I had nothing else worth hanging on to."

There was silence after he'd said that. It was kind of

profound. Then Jordan ruined it by sniggering, which led to a chain reaction of laughing that bordered on hysterical. All three lay back on the new wood and stared up at the stars as they popped into the spreading dark of the sky one by one.

It was the snoring sound that alerted them to Evan having fallen asleep, empty beer bottle clutched against his chest.

"You're not such a dick, I guess," Jordan finally said bravely to the dozing Evan, the beer giving him a pleasant buzz.

Kieran snorted and thumped his boyfriend on the arm. Jordan caught the hand and held it tight. Kieran curved up to stand, pulling Jordan with him and guiding them both away from Evan. They stood wrapped in an embrace, exchanging soft, lazy kisses and tasting beer on each other's lips.

Chapter Seventeen

Jordan wouldn't tell him where they were going. He had just grabbed bags from the newly working fridge in the Johnson house, and together, they followed the path up and beyond the house. It was on the cusp of the end of the day. Plum and peach chalked across the sky, and when they reached their destination in the foothills outside of Cooper's Bay, sunset had gripped the sky tight. The mountain ranges were nothing more than smudges over the tree line, and the depth of the night was creeping gently into view. Kieran had brought a picnic dinner—bread and cheese, fruit and cold meats—finger food that could be shared between them. It was idyllic, even more so when Jordan pulled out a thermos of coffee and added Jameson whisky for a truly awesome Irish coffee.

"Evan is hanging around Hayley quite a bit." Jordan looked serious.

"Hayley is so not falling for his flannel."

"He bought her a teddy."

Kieran was horrified. "Lingerie?" God, that was the first one in a whole lot of Evan-type steps that would only lead to one of two things. Evan getting a black eye or Evan getting his way.

"Worse than that."

"What is worse than giving sexy underwear to my sister?"

"It was a cuddly teddy bear holding a silk rose. Just the one."

"Shit. Classic Evan puppy love moves."

"Should we be worried?"

"This is my sister we're talking about, Hayley Balls-of-

Steel Addison."

They sat idly, chatting about everything and nothing, deciding Evan indeed needed to be watched just in case, but that Hayley really could handle herself.

"Do you see that over there?" Jordan pointed over into the seeping darkness at the rise of grass that led to the lower tree line.

Kieran squinted in the half light, and frowned. "The fields?"

"Perfect position for a house. Don't you think?"

"A house?"

"Think about it. On one side, it overlooks Cooper's Bay, just over the hill, and on the other, it overlooks the brook and the maple trees."

"Yeah, a good place."

Jordan rested back on his elbows, drinking in the sight of Kieran waving his arms animatedly as he created a house in his head. He didn't think he'd ever seen anything as beautiful as Kieran animated with the passion of possibilities.

"A veranda that wraps the whole house, somewhere to sit, to watch sunsets like this." He inched closer on the blanket. "I used to sit up here before. Sketching the Johnson house for my assignment, then later just because I loved the beauty of it."

"Is this where you went with the sketchbook on that old red bike?" Jordan had often wondered where Kieran went.

Kieran smiled. "Yeah. I wanted to build a house on this hill someday. Set down roots. A house that digs deep into the land, looks like it's been there for a hundred years, maybe a painted lady."

"But your future seemed to be in London." Jordan was always the realist. How could Kieran want to have roots here when he'd clearly been happy to create a new life in England? Kieran closed his eyes briefly and shook his head.

"I want to sit outside, Jordan, and watch the dogs or the kids play, eat dinner outside with my partner."

"That is a lovely dream. We all need dreams."

"Us, Jordan. Eh? Maybe one day." Kieran sounded wistful, but there was a trace of steel in his voice, a determination. Jordan bumped arms with him. At this moment, as the sun slipped low and night invited all sorts of secrets, there was only one thing he could say.

"Yeah, maybe one day."

Kieran laughed, gathering up the containers then standing. He offered his hand to Jordan. "Ice cream?"

"Nonnio's?" Jordan's mouth started watering almost as soon as he imagined the triple chocolate sundae that had been the highlight of his teenage post-game Thursday nights. There was only one place in the small town that served the best ice cream he'd ever tasted.

"Nonnio's."

* * * *

The sidewalk was quiet, and the chocolate ice cream was melting with full, dark flavour on his tongue. Despite Jordan teasing him about his choice, Kieran's strawberry and vanilla mix looked kind of nice.

"Can I taste?" he asked, offering his chocolate cone in exchange. Kieran smirked, taking a full mouthful of vanilla then leaning in for a heated exchange of kisses. It was singularly the most erotic thing that Jordan had experienced, and his cock was pressing against his jeans as heat curled in his spine. To be kissing Kieran after so many years, on his own Main Street, clinging one-handed to the hard cotton of his lover's jacket, was overwhelming.

"It seems to me that sleeping your way through the Addison men is working out for you."

Jordan jerked back at the voice, blinking as he took in David, still in bank manager mode in suit and tie, standing under the shop awning with his arms folded across his chest.

"I'm sure he may be a little old, but have you slept with

Phil yet?"

Jordan was stunned, standing as still as a statue while the wannabe lover slash blackmailer snapped at him.

"Fuck you," Kieran snapped, pushing Jordan away none so gently as Jordan tried to hush him.

"I'm sorry. I'm sure I meant nothing by it," David said with a hard grimace of disgust on his face.

"You meant everything by it," Kieran snapped, dropping his ice cream on the sidewalk and shoving at David.

"No, Kieran. Not worth it," Jordan said desperately. David was an ass, a complete fucking ass, but people were staring from inside the coffee shop and now was not the time. He grabbed at Kieran's arm and pulled him away, blocking out anything else David had to say, glancing back to see real hate and malice in the man's eyes.

They reached the truck, and were peeling out of the parking area in front of Nonnio's in seconds. It was tense in the vehicle, but the tension switched as Kieran drove. It seemed Jordan couldn't control his temper as much as he wished he could.

"Fucking asshole. I shouldn't have fucking stopped you from hitting him."

"I should have known better. It was a good thing you stopped it. We don't want trouble."

"I don't fucking believe it, acts like he is such a pious married man, and all this time wanted to fuck me." He was so close to losing it.

Kieran used his control to calm him down. When they were home, he pulled him from the truck and guided him up the iron steps by the garage and into Jordan's home.

He steered Jordan back towards the bed, pausing momentarily to look down at him, his hands still, resting on either side of his face, staring into green eyes.

"It doesn't matter what David thinks, what anyone thinks. We are together."

"For now," Jordan answered softly.

"For as long as you want," Kieran corrected him quickly.

"Forever."

Jordan arched his neck, chasing for a kiss, his own hands gripping and twisting in Kieran's hair, finally claiming a heated exchange of lips and tongue. They were sloppy, showing no finesse as they removed shirts, half unbuttoned their jeans, then, still half clothed, tumbled back together onto Jordan's bed.

Kieran traced a narrative of kisses down Jordan's chest, the heat leaving a path of bites and marks as he chased each mark with fingers pressing into muscles and hollows defined by physical work. This wasn't the Jordan of Kieran's childhood, or even after the funeral. This was new — this man, driving him crazy. It felt new and right.

Frantically, Kieran kissed his way back up to Jordan's lips, and the kisses were longer, harder, a pushing, rolling motion between them. Desire and want so keen — on so sharp an edge that it was over before it began — bloomed as Kieran moved his hand beneath denim, unerringly closing around Jordan and setting a steady motion. Jordan pushed Kieran's Levi's a little farther down, wanting to touch his lover, wanting to make it good.

"I love you, I love you." With one more twist from Jordan, one more frantic glide of heated skin, Kieran lost it, hot and heavy between them, his neck arching as he moaned one word — "Jordan…"

It was too much. Jordan was on sensory overload. The sight, the sound, the feel of this man above him and his orgasm rolled over him until, breathless and gasping, he pulled Kieran to one side, his hands curling around his arms, gripping tight. They hadn't even stopped to think. There was no slow lovemaking, the kind Jordan had imagined in his thoughts where they mapped each other's bodies and marked possession. It was heat and need and wanting all rolled into *take now*.

"Kieran?"

"Hmm?"

"Maybe next time…"

"Uh huh?"

"…we could go slow enough for us to take our jeans off?"

Chapter Eighteen

The knock on the door was frantic, and Jordan sat bolt upright in bed, wincing at the bright sunlight that spilled into the room. He pulled on jeans and stumbled-ran to throw open the front door. Anna stood on the threshold with tears down her face and fear in her eyes. Kieran was there next to him in seconds, pulling his own jeans on.

"Mom?"

"Dad — he's collapsed."

"Did you call nine-one-one?" Kieran asked quickly, in stunned disbelief. Anna nodded and gripped Kieran's arm with a hand of steel.

"I think this is it. He's dying."

"It'll be okay, Mom."

Anna just hurried, half tripping, down the steps. Suddenly she stopped and turned to Kieran, her face a mask of grief, clearly in shock, but strength and determination in her that stunned him.

"He's not going to die," she said fiercely, "I won't let him."

* * * *

It was nearly thirty-six hours before Jordan parked the truck on the front drive and encouraged an exhausted Kieran out of the vehicle. Hayley and Anna had elected to stay at the hospital, and it was the men's turn to shower and change and get something to eat. Phil was comfortable. He'd suffered a mild stroke, and on top of his heart problems, it was enough that he would be kept under observation for a minimum of another forty-eight hours. Jordan started to climb the stairs, but Kieran pulled him back, over towards the house with determination in every step.

"Kieran?" Jordan was confused, but so tired that the edge of confusion was lost in the brilliance of the mid-day sun and the feeling of wanting sleep.

"I want to see the letter," Kieran insisted. Anna had explained that Phil had received some sort of letter from the bank, the shock of it pushing him to the stroke. She said she hadn't read it—just gleaned bits of information from her barely conscious husband. Jordan pulled Kieran to a stop.

"You need to sleep, Kieran," he started carefully. "We both need to sleep." Jordan knew his lover well, knew that whatever he read in that letter would send him immediately to the bank on low energy reserves. "We can't take this to the bank, whatever they said, when we aren't prepared."

It was a losing battle. Kieran just used his stubbornness and his extra body weight to pull Jordan the last few feet to the main house then dropped his hand, using his key to unlock the door. He was in the house so quick that Jordan stumbled over the step to follow him, watching as a hint of denim disappeared around the corner and into the front room.

The paramedics had arrived not long after Anna had come to get them, and Jordan hadn't seen the damn letter any more than Kieran had. It was actually Jordan who had found it. It had slid down the side of the sofa between the knitting supplies that Anna had abandoned in a twisted bundle and a copy of last week's local newspaper. Kieran grasped it and smoothed it out, reading the short missive and getting steadily paler until he reached the end.

"Fuck," Kieran spat out in temper. "They're calling in the loan on the house, fucking bastards, after I paid them all that money." Jordan took the paper carefully, his eyes drawn to the signatory at the bottom. David Mitchell, the same closeted and very married asshole that had been propositioning him on the quiet since college. The same asshole that Jordan had turned down every single time. The bastard that had smiled as Addison Construction and Jordan suffered in the recession. He read the words. It was a standard letter, or it seemed to be, addressing concerns the bank had that the lump sum payment made by the company, namely Kieran, was clearly a last ditch attempt, and that there would be no more in reserve to ride the repayments.

"They can't do this," Jordan said bleakly. "We have the house almost there now. We're clearing a good eighty K on that. What the fuck?" He looked up to see Kieran heading for the door, his back stiff and his hands in fists.

"I'm going to kill him," Kieran threw back at him, his words staccato hard.

"Kieran, wait, we need to think this through," Jordan pleaded, even though he thought he knew why David had done this. He understood that turning David down meant it was likely that, ultimately, this was all his fault. He knew they needed to take this a step at a time.

"I'm done thinking. That fucking letter nearly killed my dad." Kieran walked through the kitchen and out of the house with Jordan inches behind.

"Wait. Please." Kieran stopped, Jordan stumbling into him at the suddenness of the action.

"What, Jordan? What would I be waiting for exactly?"

"Your temper, we need to..." His voice tailed off, and he waved a hand between them. "Please, this is entirely my fault."

Kieran stopped in the process of opening the car door and faced his lover. "You tried to save the company, Jordan. This is in no way your fault."

Jordan scrubbed a hand over his rough, stubbled skin and felt his insides twist at the shame inside him.

"I wouldn't do what he asked, not at college and not when I came to work for your family. This is his way of trying to make me fall in line."

"What did he ask you to do? Was it more of that shit about bending over the desk?"

"You heard that?" Jordan felt shame rise in him, and his face burned as Kieran simply nodded. "He's said, on more than one occasion, that if I slept with him, he could make this all go away." He bowed his head. This sounded like some kind of Machiavellian plot by an evil man to get a heroine. It sounded ridiculous even to his own ears.

"That kind of casting couch crap doesn't happen these days, Jordan. He has no power to—"

Jordan jerked his gaze up and frowned at Kieran's words, interrupting the flow with an instant defence. "See, Kieran, you know that. I know that. Just seems he clearly has no idea whatsoever. We wouldn't have gotten financing from out of town banks for anything we did. He knew that. Money was given to us on the strength of our community links and the government funding the banks received to support in-town companies. The mortgage is one hundred per cent backed by the freaking house. He is the self-appointed leader of his own little empire, and this isn't the first time he has gotten payback on people."

"We'll go higher," Kieran protested.

"To who? His dad is the manager. Cooper's Bay is a small town, Kieran, you know that."

"This is fucking stupid. There are people we can go to— financial ombudsmen, people who can look at this."

"Which all takes time," Jordan offered patiently then waited, watching Kieran run agitated hands through his hair, seeing the indecision on his face. "I'm going to see him on my own," Jordan finally said simply, easing himself between a furious and confused Kieran and the car door. The anger in his lover died in an instant.

"You're not thinking of going to—" Kieran's voice broke in complete disbelief, and Jordan realised what it had sounded like, that he was giving in and sleeping with David Mitchell.

"No. Kieran, fuck no. I have history with this guy. Just let me go and see him on my own."

"Jordan—"

"Trust me," Jordan pleaded, curving his hands around Kieran's face and leaning in so they were almost nose-to-nose. "Just let me go talk to him on my own, see what I can sort out." Kieran closed his eyes, and Jordan could almost sense the panic inside his lover and the anger that churned alongside it. "Please, Kieran."

"Okay, but I'm coming with you." Kieran forestalled Jordan's protest at that with the gentle touch of a finger to Jordan's lips. "I'll stay in the car."

Anxiety was high in the truck. The ride to the bank was as uncomfortable as the first time they'd gone there when Jordan still felt Kieran had abandoned his family, and when Kieran was trying hard not to come on to his dead brother's lover. So much had happened since then, and Jordan was not letting *his* family lose the house. Jordan drove while Kieran, stressed and exhausted, was on his cell to his mom, exchanging information about Phil and promising to bring some things from home. He didn't give away the fact that they were on their way to the bank, and for that, Jordan was relieved. He didn't need Anna following them in to try to sort out this mess.

It had been four times that Jordan had turned down the weasel that was David Mitchell. The first had been just before graduation, which Jordan had laughed off as not going to happen considering he was with Brad. The second had been a few days after Brad's funeral, wrapped in condolences and false smiles, the same day that Kieran and he had kissed. The third? Well, that had been the time he'd gone to the bank for an overdraft. Just enough to tide over the company because the building company they were subcontracted to had gone under owing them nearly twenty-three thousand dollars. Jordan hadn't asked for much. He'd only wanted to carry over four thousand for three weeks, and David was *oh so damn* agreeable. Only his currency was in him getting what he wanted. Jordan.

He'd barely made it out of that one untouched. Then there was the last time, with Kieran in the next room, a last ditch attempt by David to get Jordan into bed.

Kieran and he may have promised honesty, but if Kieran knew all the tiny details, then Jordan thought David's life may well be at risk. What Kieran didn't know at this point wouldn't hurt him, and as they pulled into the bank lot, Jordan had to stop himself from blurting it all out, knowing his boyfriend would literally lose it here and now.

Kieran leaned to the left slightly, bumping shoulders with him, and Jordan just pulled him closer for a kiss. A kiss that hopefully would see him through the next few minutes.

Jordan removed his phone from the charging cradle and peered at the display for the time.

"I'm not having him compromise you for this," Kieran announced dramatically, and Jordan snorted at the words. They sounded as exaggerated and wild as his own thoughts had been before he settled his head to what he was trying to achieve here.

"Seriously? Compromised? I'm not some swooning Victorian lady — I can take care of myself."

"If you're not out in fifteen minutes then I'm coming in." Kieran was fierce, and Jordan kissed away Kieran's frown and declaration of intent. In a smooth movement, he slipped off the belt and was outside the cab before Kieran could say anything else.

Chapter Nineteen

David Mitchell completed the last of the papers on the Smith farm, a satisfied smile on his face. He had met his dad's quota for debt collections this week, and that made Dad one very happy man.

A knock came on his door, and his secretary leaned around the edge. "Mr Jordan Salter is in reception for you, sir. He said you would know what it was concerning."

David smiled inwardly, then he had the immediate concern about whether Salter was here on his own. "Is Kieran Addison with him?"

"No, sir, he seems quite alone."

"Show him in."

He sat upright in his chair, straightening his tie and reaching into his desk drawer to pull the papers out for Addison Construction. When he had filed to foreclose, it had been such a satisfying feeling. To be honest, he had manipulated the figures somewhat, in addition to which he may have suggested a less than stellar future for the company to his dad. But, when he'd got the signature on the procedure papers, he knew he had a way to finally get rid of the itch that was Jordan Salter. It was awkward timing, and he chose not to think about Addison senior in the hospital. That was just unfortunate. Nothing more. Nothing to do with him. Anyway, to be honest, it would make matters simpler if he could just deal with the son, who didn't seem altogether in charge of the company at all.

There was another knock. He waited a minute, the delicious trickle of triumph working through his body.

"Come." He was freaking hard as anything under his desk,

the lust that fuelled him, lust for Salter, lust for power and success, sending blood south in a rush. This was so damn perfect he couldn't have planned it better. His secretary let in a very serious-faced Jordan, who thanked her then stood in front of the desk, waiting for the door shut to signal she had left, David guessed.

"David," Jordan acknowledged, placing the single sheet of bank letterhead on the desk in front of him.

"Salter." David was determined not to personalise this, to keep the obvious levels between them that of person-in-charge to person-in-trouble. He watched as Jordan placed his hands in his pockets and rocked back on his heels.

"You and I both know that given a week we can clear everything we owe then some."

David found himself nearly squirming in his seat. Jordan's voice always went straight to his cock. Like whisky over ice, it flowed so nicely, with just an edge of fire.

"My calculations show that the deficit in your debt profile would be too much, and the senior manager concurs with that."

"Your dad tells you it's okay to pull the rug from under us?" Jordan said disbelievingly then continued, his face serious and hard, "I'm sure the figures you used will be made available to all parties."

David sat up straight. Jordan was giving barely veiled threats, and he knew if any of the Addisons or Jordan saw the figures, they would instantly know that David had *exaggerated* some of them. They would never stand in a court of law, but then, that wasn't why David was doing this.

"Relevant figures will be made available to all parties."

"Let's cut to the chase, Mitchell. You know I will do anything to stop this, so tell me what you want to make this go away for the Addisons."

With a smile, David pushed himself away from the desk, spreading his legs slightly and resting his hands on his thighs.

"We could probably have another look at the figures," he suggested smoothly, waiting, his head tilted to one side, watching the play of expressions across Jordan's face. He saw suspicion, concern then resignation. It was at that point that he knew he had Jordan right where he wanted him.

Jordan walked around the desk, leant back on it between David's legs, taking his hands from his pocket and dropping his cell phone and keys on the desk. His fingers undid the top button of his jeans, his face blank.

David was almost coming on the spot at the thought of Jordan on his knees before him. It was a fantasy of his to get some at the bank, at his dad's old desk, but he especially fantasised about Jordan Salter with his pants pushed down and forced over the desk. David had the position of power now. Jordan wouldn't be rejecting him again. Jordan leant forward.

"You want me on my knees? If I do this thing—if I give you head, let you fuck me—then you realise I have a few provisos."

David almost lost his cool and smiled. This was delicious. He could almost taste the orgasm that was guaranteed as soon as Jordan closed his cock-sucking lips around his cock. After so many times of Jordan acting so fucking holier-than-thou, turning him down, finally he had the man where he wanted him.

"What things do you need me to help you with?" he said in his best bank manager tone. He could be professional when he knew he was getting what he wanted.

"You realise this is just a pile of shit. It wouldn't stand up in court."

David felt his stomach twist. The sense that Salter was looking for an escape caused heat to rise inside him.

"We can certainly try a court if you prefer. I am sure Mr Philip Addison could handle court time." He concentrated hard on keeping his voice level and firm, pleased when Salter visibly deflated from his confident position. He waited a single heartbeat, judging where this was going, wanting to see if Salter had a defence he could play.

"Look, David... I just want this done. I don't want any more pressure on the family. I don't care how we got here, but I want you to *arrange* for the false papers you created for foreclosure to be destroyed. No more, okay?"

David nodded, licking his lips in anticipation. Finally, after all these years, he had broken down this rainbow homo and had him exactly where he wanted. "I'll sort any discrepancies that may have been introduced along the way."

"And I have your word that, if I do this, then you will leave the Addisons alone?" Jordan prompted.

David snorted and shook his head. He just didn't get what the connection was. Salter wasn't even involved with the Addisons by blood. "What is it with you and that family, Salter? I never did understand your blind pathetic puppy-like relationship." He wasn't lying, He really couldn't understand it. It wasn't as if staying with the Addisons was good for Jordan. Brad had died, and the whole family was on the brink of bankruptcy. What possible gain could there be for Jordan to fight this? Not that he wanted to question it. God. He had Jordan Salter here in the office promising him the culmination of all his right hand fantasies.

"Do I have your word?" Jordan didn't answer his question, just repeated the question.

David wasn't going to say a thing, but the prickle of temper was pressing inside him. Salter shouldn't be second guessing *him* and demanding *his* word. He was a successful, married man with a senior position in the bank, and *he* could be trusted to keep his damn word.

Jordan leant down, his face inches from David's, the smell of him, hospital antiseptic and the heat of outside, drifting into his nose.

"Please, David, can I just have your word?" Jordan repeated, moving ever so slightly closer, one hand on the table, the other resting on David's shoulder.

Damn. "You have my word." David closed his eyes. This

was literally exactly how he imagined Jordan in every fantasy he had. The man begging David for something only David could give him.

Jordan moved, and David anticipated his mouth somewhere — those lips, tight on the head of him, hands touching him — his cock erect and pressing on the zip of his pants. So close to getting this, to getting what he wanted…

Then everything changed.

What he actually got was to be pushed away, suddenly, startlingly, his chair hitting the wall behind him and Jordan standing straight, re-buttoning his fly. Casually, Jordan picked up the cell he had dropped on the table, some fancy Apple thing, waving it in front of David's face, and he focused on the screen. He couldn't make sense of it. His downstairs brain was still calling the shots, and a phone in front of him and Jordan re-buttoning his jeans didn't make any sense at all.

Fuck. What was this? Some kind of soap opera? The cell was recording. Every single fucking word that had been spoken in the office, everything that was still being said. Fear and a sudden sense of stupidity knifed through him, and his mouth hung open as his entire future disappeared in a single moment. Finally, his head caught up with what was happening.

Jordan was pressing buttons. Was he sending the audio somewhere…? *What the hell?*

He looked up at Jordan, who just nodded, taking the letter back from the desk and folding it to put in his pocket. "You are incredibly stupid, Mitchell."

David had nothing to say. He was shocked through to the core, and he clambered to his feet, reaching for the phone, set on only one thing — to get it back. Startled, Salter pulled it back out of reach, a serious look on his face, and David could almost taste the success of getting the phone back. He clenched his fist, the violence in him bursting out in one focused swing of his hand, and he cursed as Salter ducked and feinted, the follow-through of the swing taking him too far left. He focused on the phone, on the shock in Salter's expression, and moved in again, his fist contacting with Salter's shoulder. Satisfaction made him strong as he tried to grab at the cell. He found skin—Salter's neck—and without conscious thought he closed his fingers tight and gripped hold of Salter's throat to make him drop the cell. Salter just moved back, words and curses in the air, and the door flew open. The other one, Kieran Addison, the one who had been all over *his* Jordan outside the cafe, came so close that David had nowhere to run.

"Let go of him!"

He didn't let go, just gripped harder, but was wrenched away, and he ducked at the hate and intent in Addison's eyes. He wasn't fast enough because Kieran's fist connected with his nose. The pain was immediate and blackening, the crunch of broken bone loud in the room.

"Sorted?" one asked the other. He couldn't see who through the blurred vision and the blood. They walked out of the office.

"Sir? Shall I call nine-one-one? Sir?" His secretary's voice. "Someone call nine-one-one."

"No! Shit. No." *Fuck.* What was he going to do now?

Chapter Twenty

"Are we telling anyone?" Jordan asked, holding Kieran's fist in his hand and gently rubbing the sore area that had connected with David's face.

"I probably fucked it up hitting him back."

"He had his hands around my throat... Jeez, maybe you did, maybe you didn't—either way, we'll deal with it."

"He fucked with my family, and he wanted to touch you," Kieran murmured, pulling his hand away from Jordan's and flexing the fingers. He wouldn't look up, and Jordan took the initiative, using his index finger under the chin to encourage his lover to look up. He saw misery in his expressive grey eyes.

"He won't say anything to anyone. Not since we have a recording of what he admitted."

Jordan started the truck and headed home. They stayed mostly silent as the adrenaline began to taper off. It was in Jordan's thoughts that they would go straight to the garage and up to his room to hide for a while.

They didn't get farther than the front gate.

"Kieran? Jordan? What's happened?"

Jordan groaned inwardly. Hayley he could have handled, Phil he could have dealt with, but Anna? Hell no.

"Nothing, Mom, it's fine," Kieran said defensively.

"Your face tells me otherwise, young man. Kieran Addison, you get your butt in that kitchen," she began fiercely.

"Yes ma'am," Kieran said meekly.

She rounded on Jordan, who felt his whole world slip sideways under him. "And you, Jordan Salter, I want you both to sit."

"Yes, ma'am," Jordan mumbled and sidestepped her before hurrying to catch up to Kieran.

"We're screwed, aren't we?" It wasn't a question that Jordan was asking. It was a simple statement of fact.

"Totally screwed," Kieran agreed, then stopped before he opened the kitchen door, grinning back at Jordan. "So worth it, though."

Anna didn't beat about the bush, and in ten minutes flat, she had the whole story, including, much to Jordan's shame, the whole blackmailing scheme that David had been trying over the years. She listened, said little, then finally leant back in the chair.

"I should smack both of you upside the head," she began with frustration lacing her voice. "But I won't. David always was a creep, as was his father." Determinedly, she pulled the phone towards her.

"Mom?" Kieran started, but she waved him quiet.

"Your father is lying in a hospital bed because of what that man has done. Now it's my turn."

"What are you doing?" Kieran managed to ask before he was stopped by the patented eyebrow of doom. Jordan frowned. If Kieran wasn't going to get to ask a question, it was unlikely he was.

"Both of you sit and shush. The Addisons and the Mitchells have unfinished business."

Jordan sat in silence, waiting for Kieran to say something, in awe as Anna pressed buttons then brusquely asked for the number of the head office of New Richmond Savings and Loan. What came next was Anna's temper, heat and fire, held in control by the most succinctly worded complaint he'd ever heard. After two minutes of talking, she moved from the kitchen to Phil's office and shut the door. Jordan strained to listen as his surrogate mother threw in mentions of a board of directors, the local news station and the *New York Times*, and in minutes was back off the phone and standing in the kitchen.

"What happened?" Kieran sounded worried. It was just a mirror of what Jordan was feeling. What if this call meant the case was publicised? For people to know he had been propositioned by David and that he was in a relationship with his dead lover's brother... It sounded like a Jerry Springer story line or some kind of daytime movie.

"It's done." Anna pursed her lips and nodded. "I want to see your dad now."

* * * *

The lawyers from the bank arrived in under twenty-four hours. With a simple signature on the hospital paperwork, they settled Phil's medical bills, and David and his father were summarily dismissed. No one would know why. That was the agreement for a quiet exit, but their massaging of dollar amounts and debt figures were found to go back years.

Jordan only knew this because he unashamedly dug for information from one of the secretaries they'd brought with them, a young, bright-eyed—and decidedly male—intern who'd latched on to Jordan like a limpet.

The day that Phil was released from the hospital was the day that the bank settled with Addison Construction for a nice, but not monumental, fee, all dependent on Jordan's discretion to the matter and AC's acceptance of the situation.

"I never wanted to fight," Jordan revealed to Anna as he watched her cook Phil his first real meal back in the house. Kieran was holed up with Hayley, Phil and—in Kieran's words—'the cursed books'. It was nice to have time with just Anna because what he needed to talk to her about was something that had been brewing for days. "I never asked for David's attention. Not once."

Anna tuned off the burner and settled herself in the seat opposite. She opened the cookie jar and passed one of her triple chocolate cookies to him, and he gave her a smile in thanks.

166

"Is that what's been worrying you? You should be happy this is all over. The money situation is resolved, and AC can move on and grow."

"It's like none of that matters."

"Of course it matters, Jordan."

"I don't mean that, not really." He sighed, turning the cookie in his hand and picking at the chocolate that poked from one side with a nail. "I just want you and Phil to know that not once when I was with Brad did I ever encourage the attentions of another man."

"Oh." Her response was unsettling, and she sat thoughtful, her eyes focused intently on him. He didn't know where to look.

"I would never have hurt my family like that," he began to explain, his speech impassioned and quick. "I didn't. Not even with—" There was no way he could finish that sentence.

"With Kieran you mean?" Anna didn't sound angry, or disappointed, or any one of the million emotions that Jordan expected from her. If anything, she sounded relieved.

"We... After the funeral...under the tree..." *Shit, why is this so hard?*

"You kissed Kieran, or Kieran kissed you."

"You knew?" Jordan tried not to sound horrified. All the time she had known about the single most important regret of his life, when he turned away from his lover only days after his death to take comfort from the affections of his brother?

"A mother knows everything." She placed her hands over his, stilling the nervous scratching at the cookie that was resulting in a small pile of crumbs on the scarred oak table.

"Mom..." Tears choked his throat as he realised he had called her Mom and at the stifling emotion pushing from his chest. "I'm happy, and I love Kieran, but I did that to Brad. What kind of man does that make me?"

"It makes you the kind of man who loved deeply and fought so hard to hang on to the old Brad. Don't think we didn't see what was happening, sweetheart. He wasn't happy here — with you, with us, with anything. He had grown up and grown away from you a long time before either of you realised it."

"You really think that?" Jordan was literally floored. He had loved Brad till the day he'd died, long after that day in his own way.

"You are not breaking anything you had with Brad because you have found Kieran. I swear to you, Jordan, Phil and I…" She paused then corrected herself, "Your dad and I couldn't be happier that you and Kieran have found your way together. We know you will have a very happy life."

Hayley interrupted from the door. "Are we going to have a wedding? Can I be a bridesmaid?" Her question was followed by a vocal "ouch" as Kieran pulled her ear and pushed past into the kitchen. Sighing, he dropped into the chair next to Jordan, stealing a kiss and a sneaking half a cookie before leaning into his boyfriend.

"Told ya," he said simply, "but if you keep calling her Mom, does this mean our relationship is incestuous?"

Jordan half smiled at his idiot lover, boyfriend, friend, and glanced up as Phil used the same tactics as Kieran to steal a kiss from Anna and a cookie at the same time.

"I'm not wearing a peach bridesmaid dress," Hayley informed them seriously, starting the coffee machine. She perched on the edge of the table, and Jordan just knew Kieran would go in for the kill.

"Nah, we wouldn't do that to you," Kieran started with an intensely serious expression. "We already decided on apricot."

Chapter Twenty-One

"What you thinking about?" Jordan rolled to one side on the picnic blanket, facing Kieran.

"All of it," Kieran replied softly. "David, the company, the house…Brad."

"I still miss him." It wasn't the first or last time that Jordan had said that, but Kieran understood his boyfriend was saying it as much for Kieran as for himself.

"I know." They lay in silence a short while longer, the views down from their spot high in the hills above the Johnson house beautiful as day turned to dusk.

"I had this idea," Jordan offered hesitantly.

"Go on."

"I've been thinking about what you said last time we came up into the hills. Maybe AC *should* actually invest in some land of our own, build a house?"

Kieran blinked in surprise. "You remember me saying I wanted to do that?"

"I remember everything you say." Jordan chased for a kiss at that point, and heat pooled in Kieran at just that simple touch.

Kieran smirked. "Even the cursing last night when you were on your knees and—"

"Even that," Jordan said with a grin.

"But a house would be a lot of money, J."

"It would be somewhere permanent just for us. I mean, Hayley would own a third, but—yeah, ours."

Kieran shifted slightly to lie at an angle to Jordan, resting his head on the chest of the man who was the other half of him. He wanted to have something new with Jordan, something with no ghosts lurking in corners.

"Have I told you how much I love being back home?"

* * * *

The house was finished, and the contracts exchanged for sale, the check for their work in Kieran's hand. It was beautiful, stately, the yard cleared and the windows sparkling.

Kieran had just finished a gruelling six weeks. Phil was still under watch but doing well, and the house had been pushed to the perfect completion. They had contracts on another renovation in nearby Lakeview, and Kieran had two commissions for ground-up design on new builds. If anything, it gave the company time to breathe, gave them hope for the future.

David was long gone. He'd left without much fanfare. No one in the town was entirely sure why, but the recording was on Kieran's hard drive, just in case.

Everything was good apart from one thing — there didn't seem to be much time for just the two of them. He finally took the steps to remedy that. He finagled a booking for two nights and three days at a cabin with a hot tub and walk-in shower, all in exchange for plans on a neighbour's house extension.

He sighed and sank lower in the water of the hot tub, waiting for Jordan, who just had to make one more call on the next project. Just one more call...

"C'mon, Jordan." He didn't care if he sounded like he was whining. It had been too long since... Too long since anything.

"M'here."

Kieran looked up. Jordan was there, in unbuttoned jeans, slung low on his hips, leaning against the doorframe with a smirk on his face.

"You comin' in?" Kieran's voice was deliberately lazy, smooth, and he held out a hand, half smiling as Jordan pushed his jeans and boxers down his long legs and finally climbed into the tub.

Kieran didn't waste any time, clasping Jordan's hand and entwining their fingers. It was enough to touch, and the expectation was enough to make them hyperaware of each other.

"I love you." Kieran's voice was thick with desire.

"I love you too," Jordan replied simply, sliding closer.

Kieran smiled. He never tired of hearing the words. "I never imagined when I came home that I would end up here with you."

"In a hot tub?" Jordan smirked at his own joke.

"Ha ha, very funny. I was being serious, jerk."

Jordan leaned in, chasing a kiss and staying close. "Have I said yet how happy I am that you're here? That I love that you came back home?"

"Every day, at least twice."

"I can stop if you want me to."

"Don't stop."

They spent a long time just kissing in that lazy way where time wasn't an issue, Jordan sliding one leg over Kieran to settle on his lap. The water was warm, his man was hard, and making love was in the cards.

Life was good.

Moments

Excerpt

Chapter One

"Shit, Sam. March? That's four frigging months."

Jacob Riley, all six-three of pissed-off male, slammed the door to the small conference room behind him and stamped to the window to stare moodily at the bright sunshine-filled day outside. He twisted both hands tight into his hair in frustration, wondering how the fuck this day had just all gone to hell. His lawyers—his *fucking* well-paid lawyers— had said they'd get him off, not land him with some lame-ass probation community service crap. Jeez, like he was gonna be taught anything by cleaning streets or dealing with people's trash. *Shit*.

The TV in the corner was showing some trashy entertainment show, where a very smug presenter was reporting the latest news. Jacob tried to tune it out but it was nigh on impossible—it must have been the tenth time the show had been played in rotation.

The news of the arrest of actor Jacob Riley boosted the audience figures for the half season's finale of End Game *to their highest point for eight months. He's been offered a lifeline in a county programme of rehab and his spokesperson said he's concentrating on work and on himself. Well, folks, here's hoping this is one recovering addict who actually makes it out alive.*

"It's on hiatus," Samantha replied carefully from just inside the door. "I've just got off the phone with HBO and they'll delay your return to '*Game* until you're free to come back. Remember, with Christmas on the way, we have some room to manoeuvre."

Jacob spun on his heel. His quiet, calm assistant stood holding a clipboard, a cellphone balanced on top of it.

"Fuck," he summarised. HBO would be stupid to lose him, he was convinced of it. '*Game* was *his* show. Jacob's character was pivotal, the star of the whole goddamned show.

"You're lucky you play Zach," Sam snapped. "And that Zach is a drug-taking manic depressive. Otherwise I swear they would have canned you today, no hesitation."

Was she trying to make him feel better? "Sam, do I look like I give a shit?"

"You need—"

"No! I don't need *anything* or *anyone.* They push me off the show and they'll see their ratings drop overnight. No one loses Jacob Riley and sees their show survive."

Sam stared at him in bewilderment.

Resentment bubbled up inside him. He was fully aware he was coming across as petulant and childish. But how could Sam or anyone understand what was going through his head? Sam, with her to-do lists and her anal outlook on life, sure as hell couldn't. Who the hell did she think she was? HBO wouldn't tell his assistant anything of any importance.

"We have four months to get you into a programme and complete your work through the community service," she continued. Her patient tone, measuring every word, talking to him as if he were a small child — he hated every syllable.

"No," Jacob snapped, balling his temper and his dismissal of her into that one word.

She stepped away from him to stand against the door. "Jacob—"

"No. I'm not cleaning streets, I'm not searching for rubbish or any of the usual crap they put celebrities through to humiliate us!"

"Jacob, it's not meant to be a humiliation. But it is a punishment," Sam said, raising her free hand in an attempt to placate him. Her cell phone slid off the clipboard and tumbled to the floor.

Jacob listened, but what she'd said only served to increase his temper. He could feel the itch of addiction under his skin, and it terrified him. Although he would never admit it, he was out of control and it was eating at the edges of him.

In over a year, he hadn't wanted a hit as badly as he did at this moment. Frustration and anger burst out of him with uncontrolled force. He reared up and crowded her against the door, his hand circling her wrist and gripping tightly. "Don't get all sanctimonious on me, Sam, it's not your style," he snarled.

"Jacob, you're hurting me," Sam whimpered, visibly pushing as close to the wood as she could. Her words didn't register, and his grip tightened. "Jacob. Please..." she said, tears in her eyes, pain and real fear in her voice. Something in the simple *please* reached through his anger. He threw Samantha's hand back towards her body, but he didn't move away.

"I'm sorry, but don't push me, okay?" he said tiredly. Half closing his eyes, he took a deep breath. It was the first time in their relationship he could see fear in Sam's eyes, and it scared the hell out of him. Was she actually afraid of him? *What do I say? How the hell do I...?*

"Your father," Sam said. "Your father is waiting for you

in the next room."

Jacob flipped from menacing back to petulant instantly.

"Great, another thing to make my day." Jacob stepped back, watching as Samantha rubbed her wrist and blinked back tears.

"Jacob, he wants to help. He knows of this place you can go for the next—"

"He's the one who got me into this mess, Sam! He freaking turned me in!"

"He's waiting."

*　*　*　*

"I've pulled strings, son, and arranged to get you into a new type of programme, something different. It has an original approach, and it's very exclusive." Joe Riley stood stiff and straight in front of Jacob. He'd lost all his energy on the walk across the conference room. Jacob slouched, unwilling to show even the slightest interest. "I've made a hefty donation to get you accepted. The only stipulation was that you are clean."

Jacob looked into his father's grey-blue eyes then shrugged. He'd heard all too clearly the question under Joe Riley's statement, and hated him for it. *A year — a damn year.*

Joe closed his eyes and sighed. "Isn't there something dramatic you feel you just *have* to say at this point, Jacob?"

"If I thought you would actually listen to me—just once—maybe I would have something to say," Jacob said sarcastically.

"Are you clean?" Joe asked.

"Fuck," Jacob snapped, "I've been clean for a year, and you damn well know it."

His dad crossed his arms and shook his head. "No, Jacob, I don't know that. I know what you told me, then I find you mixing with the same lowlifes you knew six years ago. What was I supposed to think? What was I supposed to do? Tell me, son."

"Turn me into the cops, obviously." Jacob clenched his hands into tight fists at his sides.

"Do you think it was easy for me to do this, Jacob? Call the police on my own son?"

"Yeah. Yeah, I do, actually." He'd long ago convinced himself that his dad had perversely enjoyed turning him in, and he chose to ignore the pained expression that crossed his dad's face. "It kinda solves all those issues around having to maybe—I don't know—talk to me instead?"

Joe inhaled sharply as if he had been physically hit, and Jacob wondered how his dad was going to defend his parenting skills this time.

"Do you think your mother and I want to be visiting a morgue, identifying your body, and seeing track marks on your arms? We had to do something, had to stop you from self-destructing."

Jacob tugged self-consciously at his sleeves, anger building inside him. He had been clean for well over a year. Why didn't anyone trust him? Jacob rolled his eyes. "Now who's being dramatic? Just because I had the stuff didn't mean I was using. You could have tried asking me why I had it on me."

"And you wouldn't have lied to us?" Joe asked simply, his voice calm. Jacob didn't answer. He wasn't going to rise to the bait. "This is your last chance, Jacob. Take it. You could actually make something of yourself."

"So what the hell do you call two movies and a successful TV series? Nothing?" His parents had never liked that he had decided to pursue acting. They'd always made it very clear that they expected him to join the family accountancy firm. He'd endured several wearying years of forcing and badgering.

"I swear, Jacob, if you ruin this, I will hold back every penny of your inheritance." *Where the hell have I heard that before?* "I make three million a movie, and eighty thou for every episode of *'Game*. Seriously—you really think your money matters to me?"

"I swear every penny of mine will go to your brother," Joe continued, but Jacob had heard that threat before too, and it had the same impact as always—no impact at all.

"That loser?"

"Tell me, Jacob, why is Micah the loser? He has a career, a wife, a great kid—your nephew. He has a life."

"I've got a freaking career, Dad, and let's face it—kids? That isn't gonna happen. I'm gay!" Frustrated, Jacob pushed his fingers through his hair and closed his eyes.

"I'm not arguing, Jacob. This isn't about some petty brotherly feud, or who is happy and who isn't. You had every advantage—everything money could buy, every ounce of love your mother and I had in us. Son, please. This is your life, and your mom and I are desperate for you to see that! But somehow you don't give a damn about it."

"Well, maybe I don't."

"For God's sake, Jacob, stop being so damn melodramatic. As far as I'm concerned, we're done talking. Go home and get some clothing together. Ben is outside. He'll take you home, then he'll drive you down tomorrow."

"And if I say no?"

"You can't. I've pulled strings, but at the end of the day, it's either this programme or you're back in prison. This programme is the only reason you're not back there now."

Shit.

* * * *

Ethan Myers was tired—exhaustingly, mind-numbingly tired. He'd been up all night with Isabella and the baby. Today he was faced with an inspection from the county and the new arrival of…whoever the man was.

Coffee. Black coffee. He'd drunk so much of the stuff through the night he was wired and on the shaky side. He groaned softly as he lowered himself into his office chair. He couldn't allow himself to collapse onto the sofa because sleep would immediately chase him down.

177

Dawn had long since passed. In fact, Ethan had watched it paint the sky with delicately muted pinks and mauves before the morning daylight had begun to break the fragile peace of the pre-dawn hour. He had watched the sky out of the window in Beth and Isabella's room as he'd paced, rocking Beth in his arms and singing softly. Her fever had finally broken overnight. Just before six a.m. she'd actually allowed herself to be settled in the arms of her mother.

He glanced up at the clock, which showed eight a.m. The quarterly building code compliance inspection was scheduled to start in half an hour. Wearily, he ran a hand over his face, rough with stubble. He hoped against hope he would pass for casually cool as opposed to casually scruffy. Scruffy was not a good look for a man in charge of two hundred thousand dollars of the county's budget.

His head was drooping ever closer to his desktop when Isabella popped her head round his permanently open door. He shot upright in his chair in surprise, his hand flat on his chest.

"Sorry, Mr Myers," she said with a wry smile. "I just wanna say thank you for your help with Beth in the night."

"It's really not a problem. That's what I'm here for." Her smiled turned to a frown and he knew exactly what she was going to say.

"She's my responsibility."

"Considering you spent all of yesterday dealing with a fractious baby, I think sleep was just what you needed," he said reassuringly. She shifted nervously from foot to foot. "How is Beth now?" It was always so difficult to get a real conversation out of the quiet teen, and he usually carried the bulk of any discussion they had.

"The doctor says she'll be fine."

Ethan waited for the inevitable discomfort that emanated from Isabella whenever medical bills were discussed, and the embarrassment that came with Ethan covering those bills.

"That's good news." He waited patiently, experienced

enough to give her time.

"Mr Myers," she began timidly, casting a quick glance up to his eyes. Ethan nodded encouragingly, and she looked down at the floor. "I'm thinking now is the time for me to sign up for some classes here," she said in a rush. Ethan smiled in genuine happiness at the momentous decision.

"I'm glad you want to start classes." He sat back in his chair. "I'll let Maria know so she can sort out a schedule and figure out some day care for Beth."

"I can read, you know..." Isabella said. "Well, I can kinda read, and I would try really hard."

"You're going to do well, Isabella. I promise you," Ethan replied.

"Thank you, Mr Myers." Isabella shot him a quick grin then left what the staff affectionately called Ethan's Cave.

Isabella's news had made his day. Ethan felt more connected to the world when he was able to care for others. Taking in Isabella and Beth, giving them a home when they'd had none, gave him the opportunity to feel like he was making a difference in someone's life. By just being themselves and letting him do things like walk the floor with Beth until her fever broke, those things filled him with hope and confidence that he was doing the right thing.

He looked around the room, at the posters on the wall, the books on the shelves, at the paperwork in its neat and ordered stacks on his cabinet. The Cave was peaceful. He mentally allotted himself ten minutes to shut his eyes, and sank into the quiet. But his thoughts immediately centred on today's meeting. Ethan hated having to deal with overbearing and condescending officials to his very core and he was dreading it. Mac had always dealt with bureaucracy, with red tape.

Ethan had watched his partner in life, and in love, Edward MacIntyre, succumb to cancer. It had destroyed the strong, vital and vibrant young man he had been in the space of a few months. The word 'terminal' had thundered in his ears as he'd struggled from one day to the next. He'd been convinced that when Mac went, there would be nothing left for him but Mac had been right. He had known Ethan far better than Ethan knew himself. Every time Ethan had given in to his despair, Mac would gather his strength, and his humour, and encourage Ethan to keep going.

As Mac had faded, Ethan had grown to recognise strengths he had never dreamed he possessed. He'd resigned from his teaching post at the school where he'd taught for four years and had stayed at home, caring for Mac. He'd watched devotion and love warring with grief, as his lover's life had ebbed. He'd been there for Mac every day, every waking moment and sleeping hour. On the inside, Ethan had grieved, but he'd never let on, never let Mac see the despair as he'd loved him and held him and stored every moment in his heart. His heart had grown stronger and warmer and braver with every day, and he'd found himself becoming more of a person than he'd thought he could ever be. For his Mac. Mac had died on a bright Thursday, quietly and without a fuss, and Ethan had experienced his defining moment.

Ethan had chosen not to die with his lover. Instead, he'd learnt from Mac's bravery and strength and had become a better man. He'd used his expensive education and searched for ways to make his time on Earth worthwhile and fulfilling. He'd cajoled, begged and raised funds from thin air. He'd sold their empty and echoing condo and buried the whole profit into a crumbling, sprawling, turn of the century brick-fronted house in a run-down neighbourhood. He took as much extra training as he could and investigated funding for adult learning. Ethan was determined that, somehow, Mac's memory would be honoured in a way he would have approved of. From a grief-born determination, he'd created Mac's Education Centre.

It had been a long three years, but the centre for adult education was thriving, in an area of L.A. that was fighting its way back from decades of decline. It was one of the areas where things hadn't been completely lost to drugs and prostitution. The residents wanted to improve living conditions. Gang warfare hadn't strangled all hope for the future there. Yet.

Without fuss, Ethan and his staff went about helping people get jobs by providing basic literacy skills and serving as a liaison between the neighbourhood and potential employers. His maxim—not that he called it that aloud—was that people can never have too many skills or too much knowledge. He realised that, while he couldn't deal with gangs directly, he could certainly deal with the fallout—from widows who needed skills, to children out on the streets because of domestic violence.

He dealt with budgets and people from diverse backgrounds. He was even known to attend fund-raising parties in, horror of horrors, a suit. But there was one thing guaranteed to put the fear of God into Ethan. He hated everything about the officials and the paperwork that policed his funding. The language they seemed to make up as they went along, the contradictory and inane rules that sprouted like dandelions in grass. Ten minutes of shut-eye did not fortify him against any of the officious rubbish being thrown at him, and, not for the first time, he wished he had Mac here to help.

* * * * *

"Fire and safety codes need to be adhered to, Mr Myers. I thought I made that perfectly clear on my last visit." The little grey man in a grey suit with grey hair and, comically, a grey clipboard stood glaring up at Ethan. It seemed to Ethan that he bristled—in a very grey way—with self-importance.

"Fire codes?" Ethan repeated weakly.

"And the myriad of unaddressed items on my list," Little Grey Man continued, his eyes narrowing as he checked his file.

"The list of items?" Ethan knew he sounded like a helpless

idiot. *Shit, what list of items? I need sleep, I need coffee!*

"I've marked those that need urgent attention. They will be items four, five, six, seven, eleven, subsections b and c, fifteen, nineteen and thirty-two. In addition to that, Mr Myers, I find you sailing very close to the wind with thirteen, twenty-two and forty-one. I'm extremely concerned that you appear to have wilfully disregarded the need for a 'No Smoking' sign on the back entrance to the property." He tapped his pen on the clipboard and shot Ethan a withering look. "Is there some reason you feel it's not appropriate to do as the masses do?"

"No, I would never—"

"Mr Myers, I do not have all day to stand here while you quite clearly are not in the land of the living. I will not have a fire code hazard on my books, and unless these outstanding items are attended to, then I will have no choice but to shut you down."

What? Shut him down?

"Why?" sputtered Ethan.

The inspector smirked arrogantly at Ethan. "Perhaps now that I've your attention, Mr Myers," he said, then paused for what Ethan assumed was emphasis. "You have until January thirty-first to rectify the major violations of code—noted in the follow-up letter from my last inspection—as well as the points I've just enumerated for you as a result of today's inspection. Further, I expect to see a plan to remedy the lesser violations no later than my next quarterly inspection."

"I—" Ethan was lost for words.

Little Grey Man wrinkled his nose in distaste as he gazed disdainfully from what Ethan knew was his bed-head hair and stubble-rough face to his battered sneakers. "I will see myself out, Mr Myers. Thank you for your time," he said in clipped tones.

Ethan wasn't capable of rational thought, but his ingrained professionalism kicked in. "And thank you for yours." Unfailingly polite until the end—that was Ethan

'Idiot' Myers. He swore at himself inwardly for his southern upbringing. He watched as the official left, the front door closing behind him. Ethan froze where he was for what seemed like an eternity, words like 'fire code', 'hazard', and 'closing down' all fighting for prominence in his thought processes. *Shut us down?* All the breath left Ethan's body in one big panicked gasp, and he started to feel faint.

"Ethan? Ethan, honey? Are you okay?" A small sweet voice and a firm grip grounded Ethan. Weakly he turned to Maria Romera, his exceptionally spirited, loyal and level-headed right-hand woman.

"They want to shut us down, Maria."

"Ethan, honey, you need to calm down and think this through logically. Sit down." Gently, she pushed him back to his chair, and he collapsed obediently. "That *ratto* didn't actually say that now, did he?" Ethan stared up at her. "What he actually said was that you have until the end of January to fix the problems he highlighted."

"He did?" *Did he? He did!*

"You need to listen more closely, honey, and stop reacting to words like 'close' and 'down'."

"Okay, okay... I'm fine. It's fine." He paused then smiled up at the Italian powerhouse he was glad to call his friend. "We'll be fine. It's a list—you like lists. You can tell me what to do, can't you?"

Maria laughed, a small musical sound that never failed to make Ethan smile. "No worries there. I'll make a list, you fix the stuff, and we'll be good. Now take a few hours, have a shower, and take a nap."

"I've that Jason Ryan guy arriving at two."

"His name isn't Ryan. It's Riley, Jacob Riley. Seriously, Ethan, I give up on you."

"I swear I've a bad feeling about today, what with inspections and having to babysit this actor, I don't think my day could get any worse."

"Well, the hundred thousand from Daddy Riley will make you feel better," Maria said firmly. She pulled Ethan's arm and guided him to his feet, out through the office door and to the base of the stairs.

She indicated the doors at the top with a casual wave of her hand. "Sleep. Shower. Now."

Galvanised by her no-nonsense approach, Ethan followed her orders.

Chapter Two

Jacob's day went from bad to worse. Even his father's chauffer, Benjamin, joined the conspiracy, determinedly driving Jacob to his fate. *I don't deserve this crap! This is so damned unfair.* He was one more bad thought away from shouting at Benjamin to stop the car so he could run into the hills, get a job as a farmhand, and avoid this whole 'compensating the public purse' crap. In his mind he could already see himself — misunderstood young man, with the whole world against him and framed for a crime he didn't commit, meets the man of his dreams, a sexy wrangler, with huge hands, a tight stomach and hip bones begging to be bitten and sucked, and —

"Mr Riley. We will be there in five minutes, sir."

Shit, way to interrupt a perfectly good daydream, man. Jacob didn't bother answering. It wasn't as if Ben needed him to acknowledge what he had said. It was his job to drive, and it was Jacob's job to be the passenger. Period.

"Sir."

Jacob sighed in exasperation. Was he expecting Jacob to talk to him, to concede to his existence?

"Sir, I've instructions to take your cellphone." *What the hell?* Jacob bolted up from his comfortable slouch and glared at the back of Ben's head.

"Excuse me?" he said disbelievingly.

"Your phone, sir. Mr Riley has told me that I need to take your phone."

"What the fuck? I'm not giving you my phone." He saw the driver inhale a deep breath, building himself up for this little confrontation. Well at—his height and built like a—well, built like someone who was built, Jacob could take on Ben any time and come out the winner.

"It's a required proviso in your community service agreement, sir. I need to take the phone."

"Shit." Jacob dug into his jeans, pulled out the tiny phone, and used one freshly manicured nail to open the back and remove the SIM. He was damned if Daddy dearest thought he was going to be able to use his own phone to investigate every part of his son's life. Then he threw the cell into the front passenger seat where it bounced dramatically and quite satisfyingly, before falling to the floor.

Shit, shit, shit. He'd get another phone. Screw them all. What was he? Twelve? Not to be trusted with a phone, for fuck's sake? No, he was a grown man of twenty-six and quite capable of getting a replacement phone through fair means or foul. He'd order one as soon as he got to a landline. *That would show them the total control he had over his own life.*

The Riley sedan glided silently through the deteriorating residential areas of what must be the 'inner city'. Jacob slunk down in his seat until he was as close to horizontal as he could get. The streets buzzed with people of all ethnicities. *No doubt unemployed and committing all kinds of crime.* He was so far out of his comfort zone and thought he might get physically sick.

Finally they drew up outside a large, lone house, surrounded by a lot paved with cracked concrete. Bay fronted, constructed of brown brick, sturdy and wide, it looked completely out of place in the otherwise decrepit area.

He rolled down the window to get a better view of the place when he heard a group of people descending the broad stairs from the front door before he saw them. They were all women, rough and loud and jostling for position, laughing as they made their way from the building. They noticed the car—he guessed a tinted glass Mercedes in these parts was probably a drug dealer's ride—and stopped and stared. Not for the first time since entering the city, he groaned inwardly. What if they knew who he was? What if they wanted photos? Shit, what if they wanted to *touch* him?

* * * *

Ethan had set the alarm for one p.m. and had only pressed snooze twice, leaving himself half an hour to shower, shave and pull himself back into 'I'm in charge' mode. Sleep hadn't helped—there hadn't even been a nice dream to relieve his gloom. As he dressed in clean jeans and an emerald-green button-down that Maria swore was his best shirt, he thought morosely of what he would have to do for the next few months. Babysit this Hollywood loser and his goddamn neuroses.

Even now, minutes away from Mr Hollywood's arrival, he wasn't convinced he'd made the right decision for himself or for Mac's. He had spent a long time at his desk yesterday simply staring at the Riley Corp. cheque Riley senior had left him.

"My son has had some problems with drugs in the past." Riley senior had cut to the chase in their preliminary meeting without hesitation. "I want you to consider a placement here at your centre for him, and I am willing to pay."

"I can't offer a place here to anyone whose presence might compromise the security or integrity of the training centre. Your son needs to be clean."

"He's clean and has been for over a year. He is, however, a complete idiot who needs to grow up. More prison wouldn't be right for him. He's done his time, and learnt that lesson. Underneath all the posturing and the arrogance, I know I still have a son, and I think you and your centre will be what he needs."

"So he made it to the expedited drug programme?"

"The court granted a continuance, and has set a date for the next hearing. A long trial would create a lot of expense. No one wants another Robert Downey Jr."

"When is he due to appear again?"

"March third. My son is a very high-profile drug arrestee, Mr Myers."

"I've no doubt he imagines he is," Ethan had said, then had shut his mouth just as quickly. He'd known that he had to hear the man out. He had agreed to the meeting, so he'd needed to at least listen to the whole thing before turning the elder Riley down.

"In 2003, my son was sentenced to three years in a minimum security prison. He violated his parole when he missed mandatory drug tests."

"I remember." It must have been a slow news day when it was printed for Ethan to remember seeing headlines concerning a Hollywood reject. Gossip from the Hills was not something he relished reading.

"He was paroled again a year later, but now he's facing drug charges again. Your facility will give him a chance to prove he can keep his head down. Prove he can work in a stable environment." Ethan had thought through every reason why he should say yes, and had come up empty.

"I need trouble like a hole in the head, Mr Riley," he'd finally said. "I'm not sure the centre is what your son needs. He needs drug rehabilitation, not educational rehab."

"You're reading me all wrong, Mr Myers. I've done my research. I'm convinced he can change, and can grow up here, and I'm willing to put my money on it." With a flourish, he'd passed the cheque to Ethan. "Would this be enough?"

More books from
RJ Scott

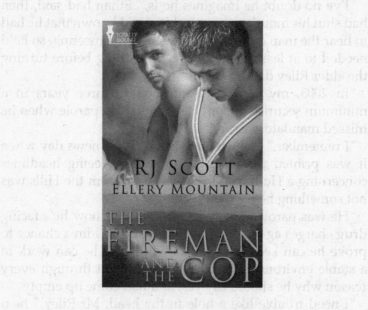

RJ SCOTT
ELLERY MOUNTAIN

THE
FIREMAN
AND THE
COP

*Rescuing a cop from a burning precinct was easy; it's
keeping him alive after that's difficult.*

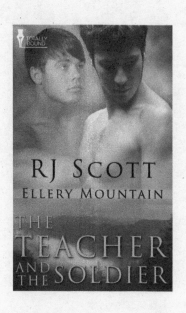

Ex-soldier, Daniel Skylar, falls hard and heavy for school teacher Luke Fitzgerald. How can he make him stay in Ellery?

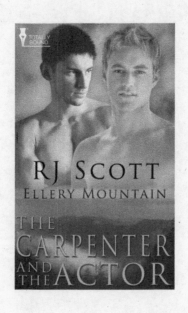

Jason is hiding and it is only when he meets Kieran that he finds home.

About the Author

RJ Scott

RJ Scott has been writing since age six, when she was made to stay in at lunchtime for an infraction involving cookies. She was told to write a story and two sides of paper about a trapped princess later, a lover of writing was born.

She can mostly be found reading — anything from thrillers to sci-fi to horror. However, her first real love will always be the world of romance. When writing her goal is to write stories with a heart of romance, a troubled road to reach happiness, and more than a hint of happily ever after.

RJ Scott loves to hear from readers. You can find contact information, website details and an author profile page at https://www.pride-publishing.com/

PUBLISHING